The Makeover

KAREN BUSCEMI

STARRYEYED PRESS
Detroit

FOR JIM BENTON

ONE

The Town Car pulled up in front of a polished steel skyscraper, the building's smoked glass reflecting the restless New York cityscape. In the backseat, Camellia Rhodes was on her iPhone, running through the day's agenda with her assistant, Marissa – an NYU graduate, bright enough to understand her good fortune of landing a job with one of the fashion world's most talked about editors-in-chief.

Camellia tapped the speaker function of the phone with a flawlessly manicured deep red nail, her signature color, and continued her conversation, pulling a slim leather makeup bag from the depths of her rose covered Valentino tote and applying a fresh coat of Nars Belle de Jour to her always-nude lips.

"Marissa, it doesn't matter if the shoot is scheduled for tomorrow, Simon's work has become distinctly boring. I want a new photographer." She sighed as she checked the precision of the dark liquid liner that rimmed her upper lids, half-listening as Marissa prattled on about finding another major fashion photographer on short notice. "Any photographer in his right mind would drop everything for this assignment. This is *Flair*. Everybody wants to shoot for us."

Everybody *did* want to shoot for *Flair*. It was the only fashion magazine that encouraged photographers to channel the extremes of their creativity. While a few other pubs allowed a breast or a nipple to grace their pages every now and then, *Flair* had run an accessories shoot with fully naked models adorned only in cocktail rings and sky-high platforms. And when Camellia commanded a beauty editorial based on a soft-core porn theme in an Ivy League laboratory, all the bags of hate mail stacked in a corner of her lavish office proved to her she was on course to change the way Americans viewed fashion.

Undoubtedly, the fashion spreads weren't all about sex for Camellia. Before the vampire trend had peaked, *Flair* had published an eerie fashion editorial, shot at dusk alongside a smooth lake flanked by towering evergreens and snowcapped mountains in the Washington backcountry. The concept was a sexy vampire with a thirst for shoes. Thanks to Photoshop, the pictures revealed pained girls writhing on the smooth rocks, each missing a foot, while the still-attached feet jutted out in unnatural positions, showing off the coveted shoes the vampire couldn't resist. It was gruesome, but effective. So effective that Vittina Mendetta, the current "it" luxury shoe designer, pulled her ads from the magazine, not wanting any woman to contemplate, even for a moment, that purchasing her shoes could result in the loss of a body part. Camellia didn't utter a word when her publisher informed her of the revenue loss. Her smug smile testified to what she was thinking: Some people have no vision.

"Just make sure somebody like Mario or Annie are on set tomorrow morning, ready to go with the theme."

There was a slight hesitation on Marissa's end. "The butcher shop?"

"Of course," Camellia replied, letting herself out of the car onto the congested sidewalk. "Red is *the* color for fall 2008."

In the elevator, Camellia checked her beloved Cartier watch, the one she had purchased for herself on her three-year anniversary as editor-in-chief of *Flair*. She was precisely thirty-five minutes late for the impromptu editorial meeting she had called just past eleven the night before. As she burst through the conference room's double doors – possibly the only person able to make such an entrance while remaining utterly graceful – every face in the room turned in her direction, the cacophony of voices silenced.

"So, what have you accomplished while awaiting my arrival?" Camellia demanded, making eye contact with every editor and junior editor in the room. She was met with blank expressions. Her eyebrows jumped. "Nothing?" Pressing her hands on the smooth granite table, Camellia bent forward, placing herself at eye level with the staff, her nostrils flaring. "That's disappointing. One would think an educated, experienced group of editors would be able to find a shred of constructive work to attend to when left alone without adult supervision."

Straightening her posture and pulling her hands to her chest prayer-like, Camellia paced the length of the table in dramatic fashion, eyes cast down, shaking her head as if bewildered. She began mumbling to herself, just loud enough to be heard by anyone trying to listen, which was the entire editorial staff, all watching their leader with obvious trepidation. "You think you're giving your employees the tools to be successful, but they think they know more than you. They think they don't need your knowledge. They think they can go about things their own way. Yes, this is what they think." She stopped abruptly and popped up her head to reveal a devilish grin. "Well I know what I think. I think you can all spend your dinners and cocktail hours here every day this week, planning your editorial calendars for next year, which best be done by Friday or you can stay the weekend, too. Meeting adjourned."

Camellia paraded out of the conference room past Marissa, who looked browbeaten with five people surrounding her desk, waiting to speak with her. Once behind the closed double doors of her corner office, Camellia broke into a wide smile as she dropped into her leather desk chair.

It was no surprise to Camellia that her editors hadn't done a shred of work in her absence, even though she had taught them so well that they should have been conducting their own meeting, going over the small items that didn't warrant Camellia's time. However, with zero supervision, that pack of twenty-somethings chose to spend their time doing nothing more than exchanging idle chitchat. Quite the opposite of Camellia at that age, this bunch was less concerned about getting ahead than taking self-portraits for Instagram and obsessively counting their likes on Facebook. Which is exactly why she had set them up to fail. Because a great teacher knows that sometimes a student has to fall on her ass before she starts using her head.

The only to-do left to complete this valuable lesson was to fire one of them. Extreme? Perhaps. But it had to be done. That pack of mutts didn't learn easily. It would take a major shakeup to get their attention. The only question was who? It couldn't be the newest hire or the editor struggling the most with the job. That would be too obvious and wouldn't have the same impact. No, it had to be someone of some standing among the other editors. Someone whose termination would not only shock but also serve as warning that everyone was replaceable.

Camellia's eyes narrowed as she mentally sorted through her editorial staff. She swiveled back and forth in her chair as she considered and then passed on editor after editor. And then she landed on Sylvia Raczka.

Sylvia had the body of a model, the brain of a Mensa member, and the emotional maturity of a high-school girl. She had been working as one of *Flair*'s digital editors, conceptualizing and writing copy for the magazine's website, and was in line for a senior fashion editor position. Well liked by her colleagues but entirely too unsophisticated for Camellia's taste, Sylvia had one other trait that made her an exceptional choice for termination: instability. The previous spring Sylvia had been arrested for disorderly conduct and indecent exposure, or so Camellia had read in the girl's file late one evening after the Human Resources department had cleared out for the day. According to the report, Sylvia had gotten blitzed out of her mind at a crowded club, climbed into a cage reserved for the hired dancers, and removed her shirt and bra. All because she had gotten dumped by a longtime flame earlier that afternoon. Two of her fellow editors, who had accompanied Sylvia to the club, witnessed the scene, which included a topless Sylvia clinging to the bars of the cage as two police officers attempted to remove her from the premises. The following morning, after posting Sylvia's bond, the editors escorted her to Jan, the unkempt HR director, for help. Jan booked an appointment for Sylvia with a therapist a few blocks from the Ruther Jacobs Publishing building, and she was still going to the weekly sessions.

She was perfect.

Camellia reached for her San Pellegrino, set out for her twice daily on a mirrored tray, and crossed the room, sinking into a hand-carved mahogany sofa set perpendicular to the floor-to-ceiling window with an enviable view of Times Square.

The phone rang, a cool, purring ringtone that coordinated perfectly with the room's silver-leafed walls and dark wood furniture with stark white upholstery. Ignoring the phone, Camellia kept her eyes focused on the scads of people scurrying along the sidewalks, their lives – and clothes – seeming so ordinary. Mothers dressed in ill-fitting denim and non-descript tops (they weren't blouses or tunics or halters, just tops) pushing crying babies in overstocked strollers. Young men in polos and khakis en route to their stale cubicles. How Camellia had feared that life while growing up in suburbia outside Philadelphia, where the great thrills of the week were Euchre tournaments and Monday Night Football. Her thrills now were dinner parties with Marc Jacobs and friends, and Fashion Week in

Milan. While her parents had been satisfied bringing up a child in a twelve-hundred-square-foot box wedged into a street of similar boxes, Camellia found the lifestyle too much like a sci-fi plotline of clones and unconsciousness.

Camellia gazed across the room at the framed images of her favorite *Flair* covers that lined the wall opposite her desk and couldn't help but smile. She had taken a magazine that was getting lost in the congested bookstore periodical shelves and singlehandedly turned it into a publication that got attention. A lot of attention. And she was certain that the next chapter of her professional life was just around the corner. In the publishing world, editors were constantly shuffling from one magazine to another. For all Camellia knew, next week could bring a new fashion magazine, in Paris perhaps, requiring her to jet off instantly to her next assignment, with no time to gather her editorial staff for a fond farewell and last-minute instructions.

She huffed as she mentally replayed the scene in the conference room and recalled the blank look on all those faces. How in the world would such incapable editors finish the current issue – or proceed to the next – without her handholding?

She crinkled her forehead, but immediately caught the bad habit and let her muscles relax. With her family's history of early forming deep furrows, Botox would be inevitable.

Annoyed with her staff all over again, Camellia reached for the phone to ring Marissa's desk. She was ready to terminate Sylvia Raczka. As she buzzed for her assistant, there was a soft rapping at the door – Marissa's customary knock. Camellia hung up the phone, called out "Come in," and perched herself on the edge of the sofa, readying to demand that Sylvia be brought to her at once. The massive doors swung open and a rolling rack filled with clothes wheeled in. "Sarah needs her final wardrobe selections approved for tomorrow's shoot," Marissa said, nodding in the direction of the junior fashion editor, a painfully thin girl sporting short, spiky hair and a one-shoulder Carmen Marc Valvo dress, who was more or less hiding behind the rack of clothes she was pushing.

Camellia sighed. Sylvia would have to wait a little while longer. "Let's see." She waved her hand and the junior editor jumped into action, thrusting the rack over to the sofa. Knifing through the dresses, blouses, skirts, and trousers, Camellia groaned, shaking her head repeatedly. "Rocker chic has been done a thousand times," she finally said, Sarah's shoulders and expression slumping in response. "I realize it's still relevant. It's *Flair*'s job to show it in a different way." Eyeing a pair of True Religion jeans, she took hold of a well-placed tear in the denim and forcefully ripped the material until there was a gaping hole in the thigh, high enough to be potentially scandalous. "Rockers don't sew. Rockers leave stains. Mutilate the rest then come back to me." Sarah stood motionless, her mouth hanging open. Camellia scowled. "Do you have a problem with my direction?"

Sarah hesitated. "There's a three-thousand-dollar Versace jacket in the collection."

"And you think it's above *Flair*'s art direction?"

Darting her eyes away from Camellia's intense gaze, Sarah shook her head.

"I didn't think so."

Sarah took leave of her boss' office at once, Camellia wondering if the still-green junior was moving so quickly to get started on her task or to escape any further – yet well deserved – scrutiny.

Even when she was a young intern at *The New Yorker*, Camellia had neither felt flustered by her highly regarded editors nor allowed her opinions to be silenced by those with decades more experience. *Those with the best ideas should speak.* She laughed lightly, recalling using those very words in her first editorial meeting. It was expected that the interns were present only to absorb the often-heated discussions that went on in the crowded conference room, but while the other interns hugged the walls, scribbling furiously on notepads, Camellia stood forward, practically grazing the head of a charming managing editor with her midriff, certain he found her attractive enough not to object. And when she stated, with no hesitation whatsoever, that the current issue's political profiles bored her, and suggested a story about influential celebrities' ability to change a generation's thought process simply because they were thin and stylish and indifferent to the world's opinions, mouths dropped for only a moment before the cute managing editor began nodding his affirmation and the others followed. At the end of the internship program, Camellia was the only one offered a job at the magazine, which she politely but firmly turned down for a junior editor position at *Elle*.

By seven o'clock, after a full day of meetings and an unusually long lunch with a surprisingly lighthearted and charming emerging eco-designer – she usually thought the "green" designers too serious and focused on their agenda to bestow amusing conversation – Camellia still hadn't found a moment to make an example out of Sylvia. The entire editorial staff was still in the building, enduring their punishment. Her eyebrows jumped: It was the perfect opportunity. She could do it *in front* of the group. That would be an experience none of them would soon forget.

Marissa buzzed. "What is it?" Camellia snapped as she cradled the phone in the crook of her neck to straighten her black and white Chanel jacket and skirt.

"Diane von Furstenberg is calling."

The sound of the glamorous fashion designer's name gave Camellia a shiver. "Put her through," she responded, careful to mask her excitement. Of all the designers she had dined with, or sat front row at their fashion shows, none thrilled her like Diane. She loved the designer's tenacity to carve out her own career – when she easily could have transformed into the ultimate lady who lunched, thanks to her former husband's fortune – and Camellia saw the resulting style empire as one of the finest brands in fashion design. Letting out an unladylike breath reminiscent of air escaping from a balloon, Camellia pressed the blinking button on the phone, closed her eyes, and said with cheerful composure, "Well, good evening, Diane."

The call was the invitation Camellia had been expecting. An intimate dinner party for fourteen a week from Tuesday at the designer's home situated over her New York shop. Plenty of time for Camellia to get a fresh gloss of red for her blunt shoulder-length hair, plus the quintessential this-old-thing cocktail dress that would have any paparazzi perched outside the building salivating to capture first. She had just finished recording the event to her laptop's calendar when her door opened unexpectedly, a mop of slicked dark hair announcing Tray Mathers, CEO of Ruther Jacobs Publishing, which owned a catalog of magazines, including *Flair*.

Camellia looked down her nose at Tray, wishing she had her chic black reading glasses handy to exaggerate her expression. "Did we have a meeting, Tray?" Her disrespect for the CEO was obvious, but she didn't care. It was imperative the young know-it-all was cognizant of Camellia's contempt for him. Fast tracking to the top of a major publishing company, thanks to sufficient string pulling by one's newspaper-mogul father, didn't impress her one bit, and while he was indeed over her on the company's organizational chart, Camellia refused to recognize him as her boss. Unfortunately, Tray never seemed to notice.

"No, but this couldn't wait."

Tray lived the CEO life with gusto, complete with custom suits, new Maserati, and eleven-room penthouse – regrettably for Camellia in the same building where she lived. Eyeing his strong jaw and impossibly white teeth, she wondered what a single man did with all those rooms, having no wife or kids to fill them.

"Fine, but I'm due at a dinner party in twenty minutes," she fibbed, hoping to quash any notion that the two might settle in for a good long chat.

Tray took the armchair in front of Camellia's desk, perching on the edge of the seat, his arms crossed on the desk. "I don't think I'll need that long." There was a flicker in his eye that instantly made Camellia uncomfortable. She hated all interactions with Tray and his lame attempt at a take-no-bullshit attitude. While she was certain it was a put-on to match his title, all she thought it really made him was an enormous douche. Now he was staring her down as if they were in a power struggle, and she didn't know what they were fighting for.

"Camellia, *Flair* is folding." Tray sat back in the chair, never taking his eyes off her, as if he was waiting for Camellia to break down, and he didn't want to miss a second of it.

The tightness in Camellia's chest matched the level of dizziness swimming about her head, and she clutched the arms of her seat to steady her, desperately trying to control her emotions, which included shock, rage, and hatred. "Is this a joke?" she managed to utter in a surprisingly calm voice.

Tray shook his head in answer. "Subscriptions are down and we've lost a slew of advertisers. We can't afford to publish the magazine anymore."

"Just like that? Isn't there some sort of warning period where we get a chance to turn things around before the powers-that-be simply decide to shut us down?" Camellia wanted to get up, to throw something at Tray, to storm out, but she couldn't seem to move.

"Sorry Cammie, it doesn't work like that." Camellia scowled, loathing the girlish-sounding nickname only Tray dared to use. He stood, buttoning his single-breasted pinstriped suit jacket. It appeared the meeting was over, yet Camellia had a thousand questions.

"What about me?" she demanded.

Tray pulled out his Blackberry and began typing, not looking up. "What about you?"

"Will you be placing me with another magazine?"

"No place for you," he replied, still typing.

They both looked startled when Camellia's small hand hit the desk with a loud bang. "How can there be no place for me? How is that possible? Doesn't anyone understand what I've accomplished at *Flair* over the last six years?"

Exhaling noisily, Tray tucked his Blackberry into his inside jacket pocket and glared at Camellia. "In six years, *Flair* lost a third of its advertisers. A third, Camellia. I think it's safe to say we're completely aware of what you've accomplished."

No one was left in the *Flair* offices – save for a janitorial crew, who were vacuuming and emptying trash cans as if there would be people to crumb on the floors and dispose of Styrofoam containers come morning – when Camellia finally emerged from her office. Everything looked different. The concrete floors, which had always appeared a mix of cool eggplant tones, now looked undeniably gray and flat. The once-thought chic glass desks, used by the bank of editorial assistants, were now a glaringly bad idea of greasy fingerprints. Even the towering receptionist area, stationed across from the elevators, looked more like a tacky throne room rather than the imposing entrance it was meant to be.

Camellia shook her head at the incongruous sight. And then she smiled. She had been right; her next chapter *was* just around the corner. In fact, it was right in front of her, waiting for her to swoop down upon it and claim it her own.

Sharply inhaling, Camellia stepped back into her office, took a long, final look, then headed out into the crisp fall night.

TWO

The silk drapes were already drawn in the apartment's main rooms by the time Camellia finally arrived home. The day's mail was laid out on the mahogany sofa table, but Camellia ignored it, instead peeking into the kitchen to make sure the cook had left for the day. She had no energy for pleasantries or common courtesy, and though she had never "gone off" on the staff – as she had often witnessed her famous photographer friend Sylvia Steiner do – this surely would have been the day, had any of them been present.

Once she was certain they had all gone home, Camellia screamed – loud, long lamenting. It wasn't a planned reaction. She hadn't felt it coming. It just happened. And when she finally stopped, what felt like days later, she noticed her husband standing in front of her, pale as snow.

Camellia woke with a start, rising quickly into the morning's diffused light before her stomach jerked and every muscle tensed, and she lay back down again, remembering the previous evening. The house was already buzzing with activity. Alain, the cook, was clanging about in the kitchen, making far too much noise considering the time of day. Camellia twisted her head, just enough to get a view of the clock. Six-thirty. Instinct urged her to get up and do something productive, but she couldn't think of a single thing that required her efforts. Every moment of her life for the last six years had been dedicated to *Flair*. She didn't know anything else.

The door handle turned and Camellia braced herself, not wanting Alain to see (and then gossip about) her current state. Usually, by this time of the morning, Camellia was already worked out and showered, wrapped in a silk robe and prepping her skin for makeup when Alain would deliver her customary breakfast of egg whites, fresh fruit, and green tea. She breathed a resounding sigh of relief as Henry's crop of white-blond hair appeared in the doorway. He was armed with *The New York Times* and her breakfast tray. "Morning Sweetie," he said a little too brightly.

"Hi," she managed, her throat surprisingly sore. She propped herself up on the generous down pillows covered in crisp white Egyptian cotton linens. The strap of her silk nightgown slid down one shoulder, and Camellia swiftly caught it and put it back in its place. She nodded slightly, and Henry, as if on cue, placed the tray on her lap and then took a seat on the edge of the bed.

"Wasn't sure if you much cared about reading *The Times* this morning," Henry said.

"I'm sure it's safe," Camellia replied, lifting the bone china teacup with an unsteady hand. "They'll have to notify the staff before a release is sent to the press." Suddenly the teacup felt like it weighed fifty pounds, and she lowered it to the tray with a splash.

Henry placed a hand on his wife's toned calf. "They're going to be okay."

Camellia yanked her leg back under the covers, moved the tray onto the bed and grabbed the front section of the paper, snapping it open to block her view of Henry. "Of course they're going to be okay," she asserted. "They learned everything they know from me."

Ignoring his wife's cold demeanor, Henry stood and kissed her on the forehead. "I have to get to the hospital. Dinner in tonight?"

"Of course." Camellia didn't look up from the paper.

It wasn't until she heard the soft click of the bedroom door that she lowered the paper, thankful to be alone. Her loss of control the night before had upset her even more than it had Henry. And the embarrassment that followed rattled her from deep inside. The only scenes she had ever caused had occurred on the red carpet, with Camellia flaunting an off-the-runway ensemble, and a flock of photographers shouting her name in hopes of a little eye contact for their pictures. Hysterics were foreign to her. Until last night.

Folding the newspaper and placing it precisely next to the damp tray, she lay back into the pillows and drew up the downy comforter to her chin. Her eyes darted restlessly around the plush room that was painted in pale hues, searching for something to do.

Thanks to an exemplary cleaning woman named Yara, who had

only been with Camellia and Henry for six months, there wasn't a crumb to be picked up from the floor or a sock in need of repair. Camellia had snatched up the young Puerto Rican girl as she stood sobbing in the lobby of Camellia's apartment building, watching in anguish as paramedics wheeled out her boss – a high-stressed environmental lawyer, who had resided on the eighteenth floor – on a gurney, dead from a massive heart attack.

Camellia's home had been spotless ever since.

She reached for the remote on the bedside table, careful to keep the covers in place. With a click, the flat screen mounted on the wall opposite the bed illuminated the room. Camellia squinted against the brightness, adding to the headache that was mounting a hefty battle. She spent the next two hours randomly flipping through channels, an exercise she hadn't attempted since childhood. The tea went cold and the food was left untouched.

At nine o'clock, Camellia was lying on her side, staring at the clock radio on her bedside table. She imagined that, at this moment, her staff was being commanded into the main conference room, the only space large enough to accompany everyone comfortably. She wondered how long Tray would make them sweat before beginning the meeting. His presence alone would be enough to launch a missile of fear through even the most seasoned employees, as Tray never addressed them, even in greeting at the annual holiday party.

She could hear Tray's words in her head. "Thanks to your incompetent editor-in-chief, you no longer have a magazine. Or jobs." Cringing, she flopped onto her other side, but unable to find comfort, she pulled off the covers and finally emerged from her bed, her legs a bit shaky as they supported her. Grabbing her iPhone from the imposing mirrored bureau set in the corner by the window, Camellia headed to her bathroom, determined to at least wash her face and brush her teeth before the day got any older.

The cold water on her face was welcoming, and made her feel alert enough to begin her morning beauty routine, an intricate number of steps and high-end products, proven to keep her skin firm, soft, and nearly wrinkle-free. She sat at her vanity, her legs crossed elegantly off the side of the cushioned bench, as she pulled the products from a wide drawer and lined them across the counter. The thought of a good soak in the tub popped into her head, and she gave way to the idea, having an entire day to pass with nothing to do. As she stood to draw her bath, the phone rang, and in a rush of anxiety to answer, she knocked over the anti-aging serum she ordered twice a year from Paris, the precious contents spilling onto the white marble countertop.

"Damn." She righted the bottle with a shaky hand while reaching for the phone with the other, knowing before she looked that it would be Marissa. She pressed the answer button and placed the call on speaker, suddenly not certain she had the strength to hold the phone to her ear.

"Well?" It was the only greeting that made sense. Pleasantries would be demeaning. Feigning ignorance would be a full-forced slap in the face.

"Oh, Camellia." And Marissa's sobbing ensued.

With careful focus on discerning Marissa's words through the anguished lamenting, Camellia was able to piece together how the morning had unfolded at *Flair*. Tray had ordered Tavi (the leggy receptionist with the well-edited shoes was how Camellia had differentiated her) to arrive at the office a half hour early to flag all the employees to the main conference room. And he did make them wait, for thirty-four minutes, according to Marissa. No coffee or pastries had been laid out. Not even a pitcher of water and paper cups. The rumors swirling around the room were thicker than the sweat that was also accumulating, with the number-one suspicion growing in solidarity that the magazine was being sold.

Tray's entrance silenced the staff.

He took his time making his way to the front of the room, positioning himself behind an acrylic podium that had once seemed so well matched for Camellia, who had used the delicate yet contemporary lectern to deliver her favorite fan mail selections, her petite frame erect yet energized as she had read the vernacular letters of art students and emerging photographers. Now, Tray not only overwhelmed the clear podium with his opposing stature, he also looked as if he placed himself in the one spot where he could not hide from the staff. An obvious adjustment of his male anatomy temporarily displaced the man known for the swooping terror he customarily delivered with satisfaction to the executives of Ruther Jacobs Publishing.

He flipped on the microphone, though the quiet was so extreme, a whisper could have been comprehended at the back of the room. "I'll make this quick," he said, without emotion, his eyes landing just over the heads of the tallest employees. "Camellia Rhodes has been relieved of her duties. As of today, *Flair* is shuttered. Sales reps will stay on temporarily to reconcile their accounts. A few of you will receive offers for other positions within the company. As for the rest of you, Ruther Jacobs Publishing does not provide recommendation letters. Please clean out your desks immediately. Security is waiting to check your belongings and escort you out of the building."

It was over.

"Honey, are you in here?"

Camellia woke with a start and immediately grabbed the left side of her neck, which was throbbing. The bathroom lights flicked on. She shut her eyes in protest.

"What are you doing in here?" Henry's hands were on his wife's shoulders, gently pulling her from a most uncomfortable position where she had fallen asleep with the left side of her face pressed against the hard countertop.

"My neck," Camellia cried out, her hand clutching at the pain. At last upright on her vanity bench, and her eyes now adjusted to the light, Camellia regarded herself in the mirror and gasped.

"You've been crying," Henry said, running a plush washcloth under cold water then wringing it out and placing it on Camellia's forehead.

She put her hand over his and let it linger there for a moment before taking charge of the washcloth, moving its position south to her burning eyes. "Marissa called."

"Oh." Henry picked up the house phone mounted on the wall beside the vanity "Yara, please bring up two glasses of chardonnay, thank you."

"I don't want a drink."

"Humor me, okay?"

Within minutes there was a knock at the bedroom door. Henry excused himself and quickly reemerged with two stemless wine glasses filled nearly to the rim. Without removing the washcloth from her eyes, Camellia took a long drink of the crisp, dry wine, her eyes closed in appreciation. "That is good," she admitted. "I suppose I should listen to you more often."

Henry chuckled. "Let's not start talking crazy."

Camellia smiled for the first time that day. She let the washcloth drop into her lap. "Henry," she said, her voice cracking. "What would I do without you?"

Henry clinked her glass with his. "I hope you never figure that out."

THREE

The day's multi-hour nap proved to be a key player in upsetting Camellia's circadian clock. After listening to the rhythm of Henry's soft snoring for more than an hour, she finally slipped out of bed, tied her silk robe at the waist, and for the first time in a day, left the safety of her chambers for other – uninhabited – rooms of the apartment.

The imposing modern living room with stark-white furniture and impossibly high ceilings was dark save for a slice of moonlight cutting across the espresso stained hardwood floor from a gap in the heavy drapery. Camellia pushed the velvet window dressing aside, taking in the widespread view of Central Park – the singular factor for her selection of this pre-war apartment building after only three months of paychecks from *Flair*.

The sleepy town of Harleysville where she grew up had had such a park – on a much smaller scale – where her parents took her most Sundays. "Outdoorsy people," as Camellia often referred to her parents, Tom and Gina Gryzbowski had practically raised their only daughter in the open air. Family outings were traveled on bike, meals were often eaten on a red-checked blanket in their yard, and the park was their main attraction. From baseball games to leisurely walks on the trails, taking in birds and small critters, that park was Camellia's point of reference for her childhood. Which was why she found it so funny that she would want to be reminded of it daily in her New York high rise. Leaving that neighborhood had been her goal since the age of thirteen, when she first saw a copy of *Vogue* at the salon in town.

She let the drape fall and exited the room, passing through the dining room with its mammoth round table and Murano crystal chandelier on her way to the kitchen. She was famished.

The kitchen, for as little time as she spent in there, was her favorite room in the house. She loved the stainless-steel appliances, the gourmet range with seven burners and the concrete counters. Six low-back leather barstools – which Camellia had never used – lined the large island. Her meals were customarily served to her in either the dining room or at the cozy table in the conservatory located off the library.

Thankfully the fridge was stocked. Camellia retrieved storage containers filled with turkey breast and new potatoes, a tomato-basil salad, and something with couscous. She ripped off the lids and dove in, not bothering to take pleasure in the aromas and textures and flavors of the dishes as she usually would. Instead she ate without thinking, practically without breathing, until she emptied every container.

Henry found his wife the next morning, her body folded over the rounded arm of the floral settee in the conservatory. "Camellia, what are you doing out here?" he asked, running a hand along her smooth neck. "Was I snoring?"

Camellia opened an eye and then closed it again. She groaned, already feeling pain in her back from her awkward sleeping position. "Oh hell, I need aspirin," she said, her hand pressed into the small of her back. She slowly righted herself, wondering why it felt like she had aged twenty years in twenty-four hours.

Henry sat beside her and Camellia nestled her head into his chest. "You're going to be fine," he said soberly.

"Yes I will," she said authoritatively. "I needed a day to assimilate is all. This is a big city and there are dozens of magazines that would kill for my direction. I'll shower and dress then make a couple of calls."

"That's my girl," Henry said, hugging his wife close.

"Enough about me," Camellia said, looking up at her handsome husband, "what do you have going on today?"

"Hospital all day. Can you believe I'll be finished with my fellowship in three months?"

"And then I can brag to the girls back home that I'm married to a doctor," she said with a smirk.

"Girls back home? Have you decided to renew childhood friendships?" Henry teased.

"Are you kidding? Our mailbox would be filled with invites for chili cook offs and road rallies."

Henry laughed. "You really are terrible. But I love you madly."

"No, I'm honest. And," she paused, squeezing her husband's hand, "I'm so proud of you, Henry."

He smiled and kissed Camellia's forehead. "It's still early. Alain won't be here for another twenty minutes. Would you like me to make some eggs?"

Camellia's hand went to her stomach. "Good God, no."

Henry's mouth dropped open, a sly smile forming. "Camellia, you're not…"

"Absolutely not," she snapped. "I'm without a job, not my faculties."

Feeling much like her old self in a red Donna Karan pantsuit and Chanel slingbacks, Camellia sat at the desk in the wood-paneled office she shared with Henry, her iPhone in hand. She was scrolling through the phone's address book, determining the order of magazine publishers she wished to call. As editor-in-chief was the only title she would accept, she knew better than to contact the magazines with beloved figureheads already in that role. Obviously, no one was going to fire Anna Wintour to give her a job, though Camellia thought that was just the kind of move that would invigorate the no-surprises glossy.

Jean Kingston over at *Woman*, however, was a different story. She was a too-young editor-in-chief of a rather artistic fashion and beauty magazine, who fell into the position after her predecessor Valerie Brown quit on a whim to marry Italian Indy Car driver Rudy Vianelli and travel around the world. While the adventure would be fun for a while, Camellia felt certain the move had been a huge mistake, and she was right. Less than six months into the marriage, Valerie discovered her new husband was having not one but three affairs, learning about his trysts through a YouTube video made by one of the mistresses, who was feeling betrayed after he brought all three women together in Brazil for a weekend-long orgy.

Valerie was out of a job and out of a marriage. It was rumored she had taken up with a billionaire playboy, who had no long-term plans for her, but kept her name in the headlines, which suited Valerie for the time being.

Meanwhile Jean was in a constant state of panic, struggling to stay on top of all her new responsibilities and not look like a cat immersed in water while doing it.

Camellia tapped the number of *Woman*'s publisher, Clinton Cavanaugh, and put the phone on speaker.

"Mr. Cavanaugh's office, Ruth speaking. How many I assist you?"

"Ruth dear, it's Camellia Rhodes. Is Clinton in?"

"Um, I'm not sure if he's in the office yet. Hold one moment please."

An instrumental of the B-52's Love Shack blared from the phone's speaker. "You know if he's in, darling," Camellia said to the music. "His office is located directly behind your chair."

The music cut off abruptly as Ruth came back on the line. "Um,

I'm sorry Miss Rhodes, Mr. Cavanaugh is in a meeting."

"How about voicemail?"

"No voicemail. I can take a message if you like."

Camellia paused, wanting to be harsh but knowing Ruth was the gatekeeper to Clinton. "Ask him to call me. Please. On my cell. He has the number."

By the time Henry returned home from the hospital, Camellia had called twelve publishers and spoke with no one higher than their executive assistants. She shrugged it off and accepted her husband's dinner invitation to Bacco, their favorite Italian restaurant on the Upper East Side.

Camellia changed for the event into a Diane von Furstenberg wrap dress with a plunging neckline. The dress reignited her excitement for the designer's dinner party the following week. She still needed to shop and visit her hairdresser prior to the party. Once she made some headway with the publishers in the morning, she would hit the boutiques.

The driver was waiting at the curb as Camellia and Henry emerged from their building, Henry looking sleek in a gray Armani suit, his hair freshly cut. Helping his wife into the car first, Henry slid in next to her, looking for a kiss, but she was too fixated on what was out the window to comply. He followed her gaze to see Tray Mathers entering the building. Their building. Henry placed a hand on Camellia's, which was trembling, but she pulled away.

"That bastard had to move into *my* building," Camellia sneered. "Hundreds of high rises in this city and his pompous ass had to have this one." She pushed herself into the corner of the car using a silver Manolo stiletto to get a better view of her former boss, whose imposing frame humbled the façade's ornate double doors.

"Forget him," Henry said. "He'll lose interest in this place and move on, just as he's lost interest in every woman he's taken through those doors."

Snickering over Tray's "conquests" had been a ritual for Camellia and Henry. Upon returning home from Sunday breakfasts, they had often caught model-pretty girls in designer clothes and ruffled hair doing the walk of shame from their building into Tray's waiting car. While the driver could whisk the women away, their indiscretion stayed thick in the air.

"No he won't. He'll stay for no other reason than to torture me. That would be so Tray."

Henry turned back to Camellia, this time catching one of her still-shaking hands and holding onto it. "Let's try to enjoy our evening, okay? Tray Mathers has no hold over you. Besides, if you really hate living in the same building as him, *we* can move."

Camellia sat forward on the leather seat, staring intently at her husband. "Henry, that man will never make me leave the home I love. Never. I wouldn't give him the satisfaction."

Henry brought Camellia's hand up to his mouth and kissed it softly. "Bravo, darling."

A superb dish of cavatelli and two glasses of pinot had Camellia feeling downright merry. Henry entertained her with stories of his Chief of Staff, who in full-fledged mid-life crisis was driving to work daily in his new Aston Martin, his mistress – an administrative assistant – seated beside him, singing hip-hop songs over the booming bass. After dinner, Camellia and Henry took a stroll along 5th Avenue, enjoying the warm, fall evening. Camellia slipped her hand into Henry's. He stopped and pulled her in close, kissing her deeply. She embraced him, breathing in the fresh scent of his aftershave – Henry never wore cologne, which was fine by her – and opened her eyes, curious if their PDA was garnering attention on the busy New York sidewalk. She caught site of a newsstand a few feet away and froze.

"I love you, Camellia," Henry whispered, pressing her in closer. His declaration was met with silence. "Are you listening to me," he teased, "or have you dozed off from the cavatelli?"

"I want to go home. Now."

Henry pulled away from her, looking puzzled. She was pale. Her expression pained. "What's wrong?" She nodded softly in the direction behind him. He turned and then cringed at the *NY Scenes* headline:

Flair *Folds; Camellia Rhodes Shocked*
(as we've been for years)

To the right of the headline was an old picture of Camellia delivering a speech to fashion design students at Parsons. Her mouth open mid-sentence, the photo imparted an image that suggested surprise, perhaps fright.

Henry put an arm around his wife, leading her down the sidewalk back toward the car. "Screw the yellow journalism," he snarled. "They're obviously hurting to sell papers."

"No, Henry, I have to read that story."

"No. You don't. It's a bunch of crap and you know it."

"It doesn't matter. It's out there. People will believe it's true." She turned on her heel and walked back to the newsstand, fishing in her clutch for a dollar bill.

Henry quickly caught up to her. "At least let me get it for you." He stepped in front of her, handed the man behind the counter a fifty, and took the whole lot.

Camellia smirked. "Always taking care of me, aren't you?"

"And I always will. Now let's get the hell out of here."

FOUR

The next morning, alone in bed, Camellia read the story again.

> *After six years as editor-in-chief of the*
> *oft-controversial fashion rag* Flair,
> *Camellia Rhodes' reign of terror is over.*
> *Quite literally.*
> *While the well-heeled headmistress'*
> *crotchety demeanor certainly played a role,*
> *crotches — and lots of them — along with*
> *disjointed arms, missing feet and other imagery*
> *dark enough to take over one's dreams for*
> *nights on end appeared to be too much for*
> *advertisers. On Monday,* Flair *was shuttered,*
> *and Rhodes, along with most of her staff, was*
> *shown the door.*
> *We here at* NY Scenes *will never forget*
> *an all-white apparel editorial highlighted by*

sliced skin dripping blood and bruised
cheekbones titled "Red, White & Blue" that
timed out (not so) fittingly with Independence
Day.

    Now that Flair *is just a fading night*
terror, what will Camellia Rhodes do next?
Gravedigger? Taxidermist? So many
options, really.

She closed the paper and slept until dinner.

"It's not a newspaper, it's a gossip rag," Marissa said brightly between sips of iced tea. "Everyone knows credibility isn't *NY Scenes'* strong suit."

Camellia peered around the lively cafe situated in the heart of Soho. The small space, covered with oversized Parisian posters and mismatched mirrors, was filled nearly to capacity with families dressed in jeans or cargos and T-shirts, shoveling back enormous plates of eggs, bacon, pancakes, and potatoes. The noise level was surprising, considering almost every mouth was filled. Even more surprising: not a single person recognized her. Camellia felt a sudden affection for tourists.

While grateful for Marissa's unexpected invitation for breakfast – the first time Camellia had dined with her former assistant – she was hesitant to go out in public only a day after making the front page of that nasty tabloid. But the truth was, it was the only invitation she had received since *Flair* folded. And she needed news. Any news.

In fact, Marissa had been the only person to make contact with her. Not one publisher had taken – or returned – her repeated calls. And her friends. Perhaps it was more fitting to call them the society women she mingled with at events, since that was about all they were good for. When times were good, they flocked to her, making a fuss over her outfits and pulling her beside them to pose for the paparazzi. Now, not one of them had bothered to send her a measly pity email. It wasn't as if they didn't know. For such a mammoth city, in the fashion world, everyone knew everyone's business.

Camellia took a sip of her tea and looked at Marissa. "It doesn't matter. I'm sure it won't be the last publication to have a say over me or my demise."

"It's not a demise, it's a transition."

Camellia snorted uncharacteristically, and quickly put a hand to her hair as if to smooth away the vulgarity. She set her cup on the table and looked away, speaking in a whisper. "Transition to what?"

Marissa shifted in her seat, and pulled a dark cardigan over her bony shoulders. "Another magazine will come calling. You have to give the dust a chance to settle."

Feeling her blood pressure rise, Camellia held tight to the table, putting great effort in appearing calm, although her next words came out with a hiss. "I should have been scooped up the next day. An editor of my caliber without a magazine? Please. I should have..." She closed her eyes and took a deep breath, determined not to let anyone but Henry see her out of sorts. Especially an assistant.

Regaining her composure, Camellia shook out her glossy hair and refocused on Marissa. "Subject change." She leaned in close, her face a genuine expression of concern. "How are you holding up? Have you begun your job search? Of course I'll write you a recommendation letter – not that it will mean much – but you were very good at your job."

Marissa lowered her chin, looking as if she were trying to duck under her thick, dark bangs. "What?" Camellia said.

"Tray offered me a position at *Food*," she mumbled, not making eye contact.

Camellia straightened, her mind reeling. "Oh, Jeanine lost her assistant? Well, that's great for you. Really great. You'll like Jeanine. Mind you, she does talk about the latest kitchen gadgets, *all day long*, but she's the good sort, and if you don't mind weeding through the piles on her desk to find the memo she'll swear she never received… What?"

Marissa was positively squirming.

"Spit it out."

"I'm not Jeanine's assistant. I'm her assistant editor."

Camellia froze. "Tray gave you a promotion," she finally said. It wasn't so much a question as it was something to ponder out loud.

"Yes."

"Why?"

"I guess he read my resume."

"Your resume says you're qualified to be an assistant editor at a cooking magazine?"

"Yes."

"Well then." Camellia reached for her wallet and pulled out a twenty. They hadn't ordered food yet, but there was no chance she could eat a bite now. She set the bill on the table and gracefully scooted out from the booth bench. "I mean you no malice," she said softly, picking up her handbag and placing it in the crook of her arm. She looked down at Marissa, who had managed to wedge herself into the corner, cowering as if her former boss might use her Prada Bowler bag to take a swing at her. "I just wasn't prepared to hear...well, I just wasn't prepared. Good luck in your new position. I'm sure you'll be a great asset." With that she turned on her heel and left Marissa and the tourists, plunging back out onto the unforgiving city streets.

It wasn't that she was angry with Marissa; for Heaven's sake, she understood the girl needed to support herself. And it wasn't as if she had a drop of ability in the kitchen. In fact, fighting against domesticity had been a lifelong battle for Camellia, dating back to the hot summer afternoons of her teenage years, her schoolteacher mother spending her precious two months off attempting to educate her only daughter in the joys of household duties. Camellia could care less about recipes for garlic chicken and mushroom stuffing, or successfully removing mildew from the bathtub. Her salad days had been spent under the sweeping oak tree at the far end of their yard, paging through armfuls of old fashion magazines she had picked up for pennies at yard sales, and sipping tart lemonade.

No, working on a magazine that celebrated cooking – and grocery shopping – would be a step backward for Camellia. Never mind that the position was far beneath her level of experience and capabilities. And, of course, Tray *was* the publisher, and even if he was feeling horrible about how he had mistreated her, Tray was the type to let a relationship rot rather than admit he had made a mistake. So, of course he wouldn't have offered that position – or any other, for that matter – to Camellia. And yet she couldn't stop stewing over Marissa's quick appointment. Was it that Marissa was back on her feet and worry-free while Camellia's future hung lifeless like an unanswered question?

As her driver made the turn onto her street, Camellia knew there was trouble. A group of men were milling about on either side of her building, every one with a camera in hand. "Shit," she said, as the driver came to a stop in front of her building.

"You got a back entrance?" the driver asked.

"I suppose. I'm not sure," she admitted, never before needing a reason to sneak around her own building. The paparazzi in New York were nothing like the stalker-like photogs in Los Angeles. Here, the famous lived out in the open every day. While fans did approach them, there was a more laid-back vibe to the interaction. And the paparazzi only came about for events. Or scandals. Perhaps it was because the celebrities who chose New York weren't looking for constant recognition the way so many LA socialites did, careful to shop at the stores and dine at the restaurants where the photographers were sure to be stationed.

She gazed out at them, trying to determine if the best course of action would be to walk proudly past them, ignoring their calls, when a paparazzo no older than twenty with shaggy blonde hair spotted her and broke into a run in her direction. "Go! Go!" she barked at the driver. He punched the gas, throwing her against the seatback, the screeching tires alerting the rest of the photographers to their presence. Once Camellia was sitting upright again, she straightened her outfit and checked her hair before instructing the driver to circle the area for a while. She fished her phone from her bag and speed-dialed the concierge on duty, who directed her to the service entrance at the back. The driver pulled up the car as close as he could get to the unmarked door the employees used to come and go. The concierge was waiting, door open wide. Camellia slipped into the building undetected, slipping the concierge a fifty.

Yara, whose youthful features were looking severely stressed, met Camellia at the apartment door. "Mrs. Rhodes, the phone is been ringing and ringing," Yara announced, nervously twisting a corner of her apron, as Camellia tried to sidestep past the maid and close the door. "I answer one time and say you not home, but the woman keep asking about you bidness. I say 'Is not my bidness,' but she no care. She really mean, Mrs. Rhodes."

"Sounds like she was a raging bitch," Camellia said matter-of-fact, setting her bag down on the round table in the center of the foyer. "Don't answer the phone for the next week or so. In fact, please turn off all the ringers on the phones until further notice."

Camellia went into the office and checked her personal email account. Fifty-seven new messages had arrived since she had last checked from her phone on the way to the cafe. While a number of them were electronic newsletters from departments stores and websites, pushing products, trends, and upcoming sales, a larger than expected group were from media outlets around the country. Camellia laughed as she clicked through the messages, each bearing the same request for an interview. "They won't talk to me about a job, but they're sure willing to reach out to me for the details of my *grand demise*," she said out loud. "To hell with you all," she added, deleting the entire inbox.

FIVE

It wasn't until two days before Diane von Furstenberg's dinner party that Camellia emerged from her apartment again, although still using the service entrance. It had been a full week since *Flair* had closed — more than enough time, in her opinion, to get the expected anger and resentment out of her system and get on with her life. But the get-together with Marissa had thrown her. She had expected blubbering from her former assistant, a wide-eyed fear of the unemployment unknown. Instead, Marissa was composed and lighthearted. She nearly had the upper hand of the conversation until Camellia had yanked it back with her quick departure. Or so she had hoped. She was the one facing the unknown, not Marissa. And her only chance for redemption was to make a grand showing for Diane and all her sparkly guests.

She predicted the guest list to contain the usual suspects of fashion types: an internationally acclaimed photographer, a top-shelf wardrobe stylist, a couple of currently celebrated writers, a celebrity hairstylist and makeup artist, a fiercely styled musician, an of-the-moment runway model, a leading fashion editor, and a handful of society darlings. If she made a good showing to these people, they would start spreading the word that Camellia Rhodes was still in the game, contemplating a few hush-hush offers, and looking better than ever. It would run through the fashion community like a virus, working its way through the bloodstreams of all the naysayers and doubters. Within days the electrifying gossip would culminate into a lengthy paragraph in Page Six, and then it would be gospel.

With an Hermés scarf wrapped chicly around her head and a huge pair of Tom Ford sunglasses pushed high on the bridge of her nose, Camellia made the long walk to the John Barrett Salon for a fresh coat of color and a trim from John Barrett himself. No paparazzi would be looking for her along the sidewalks. Camellia was known for taking her car service everywhere. Henry was the only person who could persuade her to walk to a destination, which she would agree to under the arrangement of a post-date foot rub – her expectation for trekking the city in four-inch heels.

It was a warm fall day. The sun ducked in and out of mounting clouds, feeling balmy and inviting on Camellia's bare arms as she strolled along high-rise-lined streets embellished with potted evergreens that flanked streamlined doors. The next phase of her life was so close she could feel a lightness in her step that gave her a childlike urge to skip a few spaces, but she held fast to her composure, rolling her shoulders back and stepping into Bergdorf Goodman, the home of her precious salon, with her chin held high.

Stevie, the overly accessorized receptionist, flashed Camellia a wide-mouthed grin as she entered the salon. Camellia met Stevie nine years ago when she first came into the salon to interview the owner for an *Elle* article on taming frizz. While she would have liked to pluck a few necklaces from the pile Stevie customarily wore around her neck, Camellia found Stevie to be competent and rather good at her job. And if Stevie was ever jittery around the cacophony of A-listers who paraded in and out the doors like teens changing classes, she never let it show. Professional all the way, just as Camellia preferred.

"Mrs. Rhodes, it's a pleasure to have you back," Stevie purred, handing Camellia a chocolate-colored robe. "Can I get you a cappuccino?"

Camellia smiled appreciatively, feeling more civilized than she had in days. "Yes, Stevie, thank you. And I'll need a manicure today, as well."

"Very good. John's chair is already waiting for you. He'll be with you in just a sec."

Sliding into the cushiony chair, Camellia placed the folded robe in her lap, preferring not to cover her outfit until it was time to color. She pulled out her phone and checked her email. There was a message from Henry, pleading for a quiet take-out dinner at home, his day at the hospital already filled with more drama than he could reasonably take. Camellia chuckled and typed, *Tang Tang Noodles and thou. Sounds divine. XO*

The sound of her name pulled her attention away from the phone. She peered around, but no one appeared to be speaking to her. Then she heard it again, clearer this time, coming from a hairstylist's station just around the corner.

"Diane would *never* take back an invitation."

"Right, but why *should* she? Camellia Rhodes has no business at that party now. I mean, how embarrassing would that be?"

"Yeah, for everyone. Would you show up at a dinner party knowing everyone in New York is talking about you, and not in a good way?"

"No way. And what are we supposed to say to *her*? 'Hey Camellia, sorry all your weird fashion shoots buried your magazine and cost all those people their jobs?'"

"Just stick with 'Great shoes.' Unless she's already sold them to pay the rent."

"You are terrible! I love it!"

The voices broke into raucous laughter. Before they could contain themselves, Camellia leaped up from the chair, grasping for her handbag, ready to make a swift exit. Just then one of the girls came around the corner, wiping a tear from her eye as she continued to giggle. She only froze for a split second before regaining her composure, which was accompanied by a snooty arched eyebrow.

"Oh, hi Camellia," she said indifferently. "See you at the party then?" She kept on walking, her long black hair bouncing merrily behind her, obviously not expecting a reply.

With tightly knitted eyebrows, Camellia waited until the girl was out of site before practically slithering back to the front of the salon, taking care to avoid eye contact. As she pushed through the door,

Stevie's voice rang out in the background, "Mrs. Rhodes? Did you still want that manicure?"

A steady rain was waiting for Camellia outside, the cabs already filled with pedestrians escaping the abrupt weather change. She could have called for her car, but at the moment, walking through the rain felt like just punishment for her stupidity. She had let her guard down. Imagined the city would rally around her for showing up at a big shot dinner party with fresh hair and a good dress.

What had really shaken her was how freely those girls – models, to be exact – were gossiping about her. The one she had come face to face with had been *her* discovery. Melanie Duerr, who insisted on calling herself MelaD professionally, had been struggling to make a name for herself when Camellia handpicked the unknown and put her on the cover of *Flair* two years ago. She immediately shot to stardom, with dozens of fashion spreads and many walks down the runways in Milan, Paris, and New York. In fact, the rumor was she had just been tapped to be the new face of Dior. After all that, instead of reaching out to the woman who gave her her first big break, Melanie dismissed Camellia like an unwanted child.

If the people she had helped had already tossed her away, what could she expect from anyone else? Shivering, Camellia put on her sunglasses, wrapped her arms around herself, and slowly walked back to the Upper East Side. The rain soaked her headscarf and clothes but had no chance penetrating the dark layer that was winding its way around her resolve.

SIX

Camellia spent the next few days going through the motions of her new, quiet life. She no longer rose with Henry to dress together and sit with tea and juice in the conservatory. Most mornings, she didn't emerge from bed until after ten. She dismissed Alain and Yara by noon so she could have the apartment to herself, the solitary confinement a relief.

The night of the dinner party had been a difficult one. Thankfully, one of the radiologists had called off sick and Henry stayed at the hospital all evening to fill in. She couldn't bare the extra attention. Henry, with his compassionate demeanor, could be counted on to put extra effort into cheering up his despondent wife. Instead, Camellia spent the evening languidly walking the rooms of the apartment in the dark, still wearing the same silk pajamas she had slept in the night before.

The next morning she woke to her alarm, which she hadn't set. It was six-thirty, and she wasn't close to being ready to get out from under the covers.

"Morning darling," Henry chirped, sitting on the edge of the bed and pushing a glass of orange juice into her hand.

Camellia waved him off then sighed, pushing herself into a seated position. She seized the glass from Henry and took a sip. "Did you set my alarm?" she asked, still in a sleepy haze.

"I did. Camellia, we're not getting anywhere around here. You're spending your days collecting dust, and I'm trying to get through this fellowship without informing the Chief that he should be more concerned with the staff than his playthings." Henry moved over to the window and pushed open the drapery, letting the morning light drench the room. "Yesterday, his admin marched right past me as I was heading into his office, and locked the door and closed the blinds. Could anybody possibly be clueless as to what's going on in there? Meanwhile, I'm still waiting for my meeting to be rescheduled."

"He's ridiculous," Camellia consented, "but you have to maintain. You need him on your side until you've landed a permanent position."

"Yes, about that." Henry, who Camellia always considered her rock, did something very uncharacteristic then that sent an icy sensation up her spine and landed in a cavity of dread in her stomach. He kicked the frame of the bed. Hard.

"Henry, your Ferragamos!" Camellia cried, nearly spilling her juice. Placing the glass on the bedside table she wondered how, in this moment of what was surely more bad news, her immediate concern was the state of her husband's six-hundred-dollar shoes.

Taking a seat beside his wife on the bed again, he put his head in his hands, just long enough to regain his customary composure. "I'm sorry," he finally said, straightening up and taking Camellia's hands. Henry's brow was furrowed but his eyes were gentle. "We're in trouble, Camellia. I haven't found a job yet. You don't have a job. And we have," he let go of one hand to motion around the room, "all this. It costs an incredible amount of money each month. And I'm terrified."

Camellia pulled away and leaned back against the headboard, crossing her arms in front of her. "We're going to be all right," she said with a surprising air of confidence.

"You need to apply for unemployment benefits." Henry's voice was low but commanding. For Camellia, the words were as piercing as if Henry had screamed them at her.

"What?"

Henry reached for his wife but she waved him away, tucking her legs under her to put some distance between them. "It's not dirty," he said. "It's what people do when they lose their jobs."

"I'll find another position," she huffed, "if not at a magazine then at a fashion house. Or with a cosmetics company."

"I'm sure you will," Henry said, his expression sincere, "But we're in a recession and the job market is tight. It may take longer than expected to land employment. Until then, we need money coming in. My fellowship income hardly cuts it. And that will be gone, too, in less than ninety days."

"But Henry, I can't wait in line at an unemployment office." A wave of anxiety rushed through Camellia, and she scrambled out of bed, feeling an overwhelming desire to flee from the room and away from this conversation.

Henry moved toward his wife, but she darted away from him, pressing her back against the closed door. "You can do it all online," he assured her. "Nobody has to know."

Relief flooded out the anxiety. "Oh," Camellia blurted with heavy breath, feeling like she had just sprinted a mile. "I suppose I can handle that." She flashed Henry a small smile, hoping to ensure him that her little spectacle did not mean she was losing it. "In fact, I'll apply first thing this morning."

"That's my girl." He took her in his arms and landed soft kisses up the side of her neck.

She was feeling slightly better. Although she wasn't yet getting anywhere with her career, she at least had a to-do on her list. Something she could accomplish. And she desperately needed to accomplish something, even if it was a small something.

"Oh, and honey?" Henry called out just before exiting the bedroom.

"Yes?" Camellia answered almost brightly.

"If we can't pay our bills, we can't pay anyone else's either. We're going to have to cut the staff."

SEVEN

Radiologists pull in a hefty income, especially radiologists with a specialty, which they train for during their optional fellowship. Fully aware how competitive the field had become, Henry had decided to pursue a specialty in interventional radiology, diagnosing and treating a variety of diseases using minimally invasive procedures. A friendly, caring man with a sharply focused personality, he preferred this niche, it being one of the only opportunities in the field to work directly with the patients.

Henry was a little late to the medicine game, having first tried his hand at photography after a college professor convinced him he had "an eye for it". The professor turned out to be right. Henry's uncanny ability to see more through a viewfinder than the typical person landed him assignments with a multitude of magazines, most notably *Elle*. While he hadn't expected photography to be a life-long career, his raw images evoked emotions that excited editors, including Camellia, who was working as a junior editor at *Elle* when Henry received his first assignment with the magazine.

Having always given every assignment her full effort, Camellia had put in the time preparing for the fashion shoot with Henry, even though her minor role on set would be assisting the fashion credits editor with properly cataloguing all the clothing and accessories the model would be wearing. Numerous entries on Henry Rhodes turned up in a single Google search, and Camellia quickly found she could not deny the photographer's talent, or his classic good looks. With a crop of white-blond hair, deep blue eyes, and fit build, Henry looked like he belonged in a JCrew ad. In most of the pictures Camellia found of him, he was clad in dark-wash jeans and soft, v-neck tee shirts, a comfortable yet sexy style befitting of a fashion photographer.

That first day on set when Henry and Camellia came face to face became legendary in the fashion world. Sparks flew immediately between the rising-star photographer and the outspoken yet undeniably talented junior fashion editor. When the shoot finally wrapped well past eleven p.m. – and the bulk of the crew gratefully made their way home to bed – Henry took Camellia to a tiny bar in the Village that was thick with smoke where they drank vodka tonics until the establishment closed at 4 a.m. and they found themselves back out on the street.

"I would kiss you, but it would never end there," Henry said, the passion deep in his voice.

"Then you'll kiss me tomorrow," Camellia replied, perfectly composed, though inside, her heart was beating like a base drum.

The next day, after a luncheon rendezvous that lasted longer than

Camellia had ever allowed herself to be away from the office, Henry moved his chair next to hers and placed a hand on her thigh, causing Camellia to catch her breath. "I would kiss you, but it would never end there," he said again, teasing her.

"Then you'll kiss me tomorrow," she purred, while her body trembled.

They went on this way for days. Each time they came together, his touch was bolder and lingered longer, while her ability to contain her desire crumbled like an unstable rampart under direct fire. A week after that fateful photo shoot, Henry delivered his customary parting line following a couple rounds of cocktails, however, this time Camellia responded with, "That works for me." That was all the persuading Henry needed. He had them in a cab to his shared apartment on the Lower East Side before she could change her mind, leading her up three flights of stairs right into his bed.

Within a month, they moved their sparse belongings into a charming 700-square-foot apartment in Washington Heights that was a short two blocks from the subway. Here they found unknown happiness, building their respective careers during the day then coming together at night, sleep suddenly less of a necessity than intense conversation and fervent lovemaking.

They didn't talk marriage right away, Camellia quietly terrified of bursting this perfect unexpected bubble, and Henry feeling a growing loss of enthusiasm for his chosen career. Though he was obviously talented as a photographer, he was starting to realize he didn't have the chops to put up with the industry. Having to baby too many entitled models while enduring ridiculous power struggles with editors and stylists were wearing on him, and it was starting to reflect in his images.

After a particularly long fashion shoot for *Marie Claire* where the model had arrived two and a half hours late, and a photo assistant walked off the set after a berating by a young, overzealous stylist who had overstepped her bounds, Henry had arrived home feeling listless and worn out. He found Camellia at the kitchen table, flipping through a tall stack of fashion magazines and typing furiously on her MacBook, her wavy, long brown hair replaced with a straightened, to-the-shoulder crop in a reddish-brown hue.

After only a year at *Elle*, Camellia had been offered a position with *W* magazine as a fashion editor. The move was "beyond exhilarating" as she described, to work for a glossy that pushed the envelope farther than most fashion pubs. Evoking reactions through fashion editorials – even if those reactions were sometimes uncomfortable – sparked Camellia. She loved how the right model wearing the right outfit in the right scenario with the right lighting told a story that words could not. And now, determined to make her mark at *W* and continue her fast rise up the fashion magazine ladder, she was spending every free moment brainstorming new ideas to take into her first editorial meeting.

As Henry watched Camellia's hands quickly moving on the keyboard, her eyes alive and alert, he later told her he had experienced a sinking feeling he knew without a doubt he wouldn't be able to shake. "I don't want to be a photographer anymore," he announced unexpectedly. Camellia immediately stopped typing, got a bottle of chardonnay out of the refrigerator and poured them each a big glass, listening intently as the love of her life confessed his childhood dreams of being a doctor.

Twelve years, and an obscene amount of student loans later, Henry was nearly finished with his education and training. All that was left was to find a job. While normally, securing a position in either a hospital or with a private practice wouldn't be that difficult, radiology had become a highly competitive field, and the recession was looming large. Not only were fewer doctors moving from one practice to another, many hospitals were scaling back their staff. And for how well Henry had done throughout his residency and fellowship, with his supervisors big fans of his careful eye and good nature, and a headhunter who had been dutifully relaying all promising leads, he wasn't getting any bites for a permanent position.

Camellia hadn't thought much of her husband's career issues. She knew he was highly capable and would eventually get a job offer. She also knew she was making more than enough money as editor-in-chief of *Flair* to carry them both in lavish style. But now she had no income and his meager fellowship salary was coming to an end. And their savings was negligible, Camellia sinking the bulk of her earnings into the apartment lease and the furnishings and the staff, plus numerous vacations with first-class accommodations.

Feeling bile rise into her throat, Camellia made a beeline to her office instead of the bathroom, certain the only thing that could make her feel better at this moment was the assurance of some money –

any money – coming their way. She lifted the lid of her laptop and typed "unemployment benefits" into the Google search box. It was time to face reality.

The following afternoon, Henry arrived home early to settle up with and then dismiss Alain and Yara, neither of them hiding their disappointment nor a few uncontrolled tears. Camellia stayed away in the bedroom, listening behind the locked door, her tears far more than a few. Once Henry showed the duo out of the apartment, Yara unexpectedly throwing her arms around Henry's neck and squeezing him tightly, crying out, "Oh Mr. Rhodes, Mr. Rhodes!" before making her exit, he picked up his cell phone and speed dialed the car service to discharge them, too.

From her post, Camellia shivered suddenly, the deafening silence far beyond being an omen.

Over the next two months, Henry cut out all their remaining extraneous expenses, including the grocery service, flower delivery, and clothes shopping. Thankfully, Camellia's fall wardrobe was already in good shape, with many designers gifting her pieces from their 2008 collections in hopes she would feature them in the magazine or be photographed wearing them. Now that there was no more *Flair*, there would be no more designer freebies, either.

Camellia was back to working every angle to find another position. Now reaching the point of total despair, she had resigned herself to lower editorial positions, including fashion director and creative director. No one was biting. Only one editor, Maggie from *Vanity Fair*, whom Camellia had worked with for a short time at *W*, took her call and astonishingly stayed on the phone with her for several minutes, graciously attempting to help.

"It's rough out there, Camellia," Maggie said matter-of-fact. "You know how quickly this magazine merry-go-round spins, sending staffers to new pubs every day. But since this recession started having larger implications, no one's moving. In fact, I haven't had a single request for a promotion or a raise. Everyone in this business is praying they aren't the next to be laid off."

"I know, I know," Camellia acquiesced. "Do you have any advice? Any contacts who many be helpful to me?"

Maggie was silent for a moment. "Have you reached out to any of the designers? You've obviously helped their careers over the years. Perhaps they could use an experienced mind for their sales or PR teams?"

Camellia sighed heavily. "Yes. It's been no good."

"What about ad agencies or publicists?"

"I've reached out to them all. Most don't respond, and the few that do all say the same thing: not hiring."

"Well, I feel for you, I really do. Magazines shutter during good times, and now, it's occurring more than ever. This could happen to any of us."

"I can't tell you how much I appreciate your sincerity," Camellia noted. "It's been rather hard to come by lately."

"I'll let you know if I hear of anything. Until then, don't be a stranger, okay?"

It had become clear to Camellia that she wouldn't be finding a job in her field anytime soon. Between the recession and her name getting smeared in the tabloids, no one would be handpicking her to start a new magazine or chair a gala or style a grand collection. The only thing she could do was to lay low, keep expenses at a minimum, and wait for Henry to find employment. His first paycheck alone would be enough to get them back on track. The combination of her unemployment checks with the last of his fellowship was barely getting them by.

She was sorry now that she had been so careless with her money. Outside of a decent 401k she had accumulated over the course of her career, which Henry was intent on not touching unless absolutely necessary, there wasn't much to speak of in their savings account. She had fast-tracked to the top of her game with such ease; the idea of falling onto hard times had never crossed her mind. And now, as Camellia looked down at her bare nails with scorn, a professional mani/pedi currently out of the question, she couldn't believe how stupid she had been.

Never one to have experienced depression, Camellia was unprepared for the mood disorder that was slowly but viciously taking hold of her.

EIGHT

At Henry's urging, they took the train to his parent's house upstate in White Creek for Thanksgiving. Camellia spent the ride staring out the window with little to say. Spending two days with Henry's family normally would have been a pleasure. They were the perfect American family. Carl and Lena Rhodes had been married for forty-one years, both retired industrial design professors now living their retirement dream on five acres in peaceful surroundings. They were regularly visited by their three grown boys – Henry the oldest, and his twin brothers Alex and Joseph. Henry's brothers had married pretty blonde girls while in their mid-twenties, and each had kids within two years.

Needless to say, it was a full house during the holidays at Carl and Lena's.

The only downside to visiting Henry's parents was Camellia's struggle to maintain her slender frame. Lena was a fabulous cook, her stuffing so good Camellia would make an exception to her otherwise careful diet, putting back a hearty helping and secretly wanting more.

Carl and Lena met Camellia and Henry at the station, both of them embracing their daughter-in-law the second she was within their grasp, leaving Henry in the dust. They had obviously heard the news.

"Sweetie, we're so glad to see you," Lena said, holding tight to Camellia's hands. Her graying hair was pulled back into a messy bun, showing off her clear, blue eyes.

"Yes, you're home now," Carl concurred, keeping a strong arm around Camellia's shoulders, his bald head and wicked smile giving him a boyish charm. "Out here, you don't have to worry about those bull-headed twerps in the city."

Camellia wondered what her mother would think about Carl referring to White Creek as her home. While she had always found her hometown confining and her parents ranch unchanging, Carl and Lena's tall white house, with a post-and-beam red barn set back on the property, had more of a retreat feel to it – a spot to wind down from her normally frenetic life where she was one of the family, and never judged.

Loaded into Carl's Suburban, the group spent the drive catching up on day-to-day happenings, Lena chatting animatedly about a fat chicken that had found its way to their back door and was now the family pet. Camellia smiled at her mother-in-law's funny stories, but she just couldn't interact the way she normally would.

"Your silly father has decided to take up wild horse taming," Lena announced, gasping as if hearing the news for the first time. "Can you imagine? So dangerous!"

"It's not dangerous," Carl reassured, turning his head severely to look at Camellia and Henry in the back seat. Well aware of her father-in-law's daredevil ways, Camellia would normally have had a tight grip on Henry's arm by now, wishing like mad Carl would spend more time driving with his eyes on the road. But today, she wasn't phased. "We break them gently. Humanely," Carl prattled on. "They're amazing creatures, you know."

"Enormous creatures is more like it," Lena huffed. "One of them runs you down and only one person will be picking up the flattened pieces: me."

"You sure are cute when you worry about me." Carl stroked the side of Lena's face affectionately, his eyes once again focused on something other than the winding street leading into the quaint village ahead.

Camellia turned her attention to the view out the window, not able to focus on her in-laws' boisterous conversation. White Creek was a charming, tiny town of less than four thousand people with a few original, yet well-preserved houses still standing from the colonial period. Looking at the town was like looking back in time with men in overalls and congenial children running along the sidewalk and women in flowered dresses shopping the farmer's market in preparation for dinner. And behind the tight cluster of buildings and dotting of well-kept houses was a widespread landscape of farmland and towering trees.

Carl pulled a sharp right turn, just barely missing the long dirt road that led to Rhodes' home on County Route 68. As they approached the house, they could see Alex and Joseph and their wives, Hillary and Amy, waiting for them on the front porch, their lot of kids chasing each other around the yard. Camellia took a deep breath, exhaling slowly and quietly, not wanting to draw attention to the anxiety that was suddenly crawling up her chest.

Camellia let herself out of the car and smoothed her Milly dress, fresh for fall in gray with black polka dots. Thankfully, she had remembered to wear wedge boots to navigate the gravel driveway. She shivered. With no tall New York City buildings for protection, the chilly November wind was especially cutting. Henry came around the car with her cashmere coat in hand, draping it over her shoulders. "Thank you," she said softly, putting her arm through his. She was trying hard to remember to be kind to her husband, who had been taking such good care of her through all the turmoil.

Henry gave her a little squeeze. "It's going to be fun."

They were quickly surrounded by Henry's nephews and nieces, the girls – ten-year-old Alyssa and nine-year-old Caitlin – were looking for the customary bauble Aunt Camellia always brought for them from her own closet. "Oh girls, I'm so sorry. I forgot." She looked just as disappointed as they did.

Henry leaned in and playfully tapped them both on the nose. "I'll tell you what. When we get back home, we'll pick out something super special for each of you and send it to you in the mail. How does that sound?" Alyssa and Caitlin nodded and scampered off, the revised arrangement appearing to meet with their approval.

On the porch, Henry's family surrounded them, bestowing hugs and kisses and grabbing luggage. Lena shooed the noisy group into the house so she could finish dinner preparations.

Camellia helped out in the kitchen, inadequately chopping at what was once a beautiful, plump heirloom tomato that now looked as if it had been put through a food processor. "Ugh," she sighed, as Lena came over to inspect her work.

"Ah, it all ends up in the same place anyway," Lena assured her, with a kind pat on Camellia's back. Turning her attention back to her strawberry-banana trifle, Lena expertly sliced through the fruit, her knife seeming to barely move as the strawberries fell away into evenly sized pieces.

"Your dress is lovely," Camellia said to Lena, trying to mask her dark mood from the family by admiring her mother-in-law's peony shirtdress that was covered by an equally attractive floral apron.

"It really is," agreed Hillary, as she walked into the kitchen, tying an old white apron at her waist.

"It's vintage from the '50s," Lena noted with a hint of pride, twirling in place with knife still in hand. "I find the most amazing things at our flea market. No one in this town seems to appreciate these things, so I snatch them all up for next to nothing."

"You've got a good eye," Camellia said.

"Well, I did learn from the best."

Amy eyed her own outfit, light-wash jeans and a cream turtleneck, with disapproval. "I think Joe would like me to wear more dresses," she confessed. "Lena, you know where I live if you ever get tired of your clothes. You, too, Camellia."

Henry's family had welcomed Camellia warmly from the day he had brought her to White Creek to announce their engagement, nearly nine years ago. While Lena, Hillary and Amy were familiar with *Flair* – Lena even having a subscription to the magazine – they never treated her differently, or used her for her contacts or perks. She was one of them; and for a precious couple of days, once or twice a year when she and Henry made the trip to his parents' home, she didn't have to be anything more than a Rhodes.

"So Camellia," Hillary said, standing at the sink peeling potatoes, "now that you have a little time on your hands, are you and Henry talking babies again?"

"Hillary, that's a private issue," Lena scolded, though she didn't look too cross.

"Whoa, so now we're entitled to privacy in this family?" Amy asked. "That would have been nice when the bulk of you squeezed into the delivery room to watch me give birth."

"Only for the first one," Hillary laughed. "Believe me, we saw enough to last a lifetime."

"So sorry I was traveling and had to miss that scene, Amy," Camellia piped up, eager to keep the subject changed.

Six months after they married, Henry began pushing hard to start a family. They had lived together for more than four years prior to marriage, so he felt no need to experience the no-kids-allowed "newlywed period". Henry loved children. And while Camellia wasn't one-hundred-percent opposed to it, building her career came first. She figured kids would come after she had made it to the top.

Henry, with his undeniable charm and constant pleading, had nearly worn her down, Camellia feeling some sense of wifely duty to give to the man who was constantly giving to her. And then *Flair* came calling. Over the course of six years, though her place was firmly planted at the very tip of the top, she had never brought up children. Neither had Henry.

"So? Babies then?" Hillary asked again, not missing a beat.

Camellia nodded at the glass of Cabernet that Amy was thrusting at her. "You're going to need this," Amy said deadpan, her routine sarcasm not inducing the laugh from Camellia it usually did.

"It's not the best time," Camellia finally said, taking a sip of the full-bodied wine. "Neither of us have jobs at the moment, you know."

"A temporary setback, I'm sure," Lena said, crumbling angel food cake into the trifle bowl.

Ashton and Aaron burst into the crowded kitchen, quashing the baby talk for a second time. "We're hungry," Aaron whined, sticking close to his older brother's side.

Lena marched to the refrigerator and pulled out two apples. "This will hold you until dinner."

Ashton frowned. "Apples? Ice cream would be a much better option."

Amy laughed, taking the apples from Lena and putting them into her boys' hands. "Nice try. Now get out of here before we put you to work."

Camellia made it through the rest of Thanksgiving without having to talk about babies or jobs or the future. If there was anything she had to be thankful for that day, it was that no one had brought up the magazine or asked for the details. While they were baby crazy, and could talk about kids – and when she was going to add to the brood – for hours on end, this was a family that understood professional discretion. And for as much as she loved them, she couldn't say she had ever really let her guard down around them. That air of confidence, the restrained demeanor – these were the traits she had projected since her internship at *The New Yorker*. Even as she fell for Henry, she had rarely broken character. It was a calculated persona that over the years no longer had to be forced. By the time she had landed at *W*, she had truly become that person. And though her shell had most definitely been dented over the last few months, Henry was the only one she would allow to see it. That was bad enough. She certainly wasn't going to go about oozing venom over Tray's uncaring conduct or admitting how devastated she was being snubbed by both the fashion and publishing communities. She had fallen far enough. How would she make that perilous climb back to the top if her protective shell was in pieces at her feet?

Just after midnight, she was finally able to slip away from the family, who were still going strong over wine and old photos in the living room, to the small guest room assigned to Henry and her. Mentally and physically exhausted, she fell into bed without removing her clothing or makeup, and dreamed of living in a tall white house with acres of land and four children holding fast to her apron.

The next day, Carl and Lena drove Camellia and Henry back to the station. "It's a long weekend, are you sure you can't stay another day?" Carl asked, obviously disappointed to see them go.

"Sorry Dad, other obligations," Henry fibbed. Camellia nodded, wishing there really was something they needed to get back to in the city.

As the train approached, Lena handed her overloaded shoulder bag to Carl, and with two free arms gave Camellia an extra-long hug. "Everything happens for a reason," she said in a low voice meant just for them. "Before you know it, you'll find happiness again. You both will."

Camellia closed her eyes and nodded in Lena's embrace, praying she was right.

NINE

"We should have sex."

Camellia had just stepped out of the shower, her hair dripping down her back as she wrapped a plush towel around her body. "Excuse me?" she responded, just as surprised at the question as she was to find Henry home in the early afternoon.

"Just because our lives are in upheaval doesn't mean our relationship has to be." He tugged playfully at the towel, which she held firmly at her breasts.

"Henry, I'm not exactly in the mood."

"Sweetheart, I can't remember the last time we got naked together," he said, continuing to wrestle the towel away. "Don't we deserve to feel good?"

"I don't think I could muster up the energy to do more than just lie there," she said wearily.

"I'll take it." Moving behind her, he began to nudge her in the direction of their bed.

She sighed, knowing she should relent. He *did* deserve that. "What are you doing home so early, anyway? And why is your hair wet?"

"My hair is wet because it's snowing like mad. Now I finally believe Christmas is around the corner." He removed his tie and started unbuttoning his shirt. "And I'm home early because today was my last day at the hospital. My fellowship is over."

Camellia gasped, clapping a hand to her mouth in a too-late attempt to muffle the sound. Henry used the moment to release her from the towel, which was met with a howl. "This is *not* the right time!"

"This is *exactly* the right time," he corrected, pushing her wet, naked body down onto the bed. "It's going to be fine. We're going to be fine. Right now is just about us." And he began kissing her from her neck to her breasts, moving lower and lower.

Camellia was surprised how excited she was; how good his mouth felt on her. She writhed against the sheets, pushing his head down until he was right where she wanted him. And then she held him there, basking in the delight of his tongue.

"I think things are going to turn around soon for us," Henry said with confidence, lying naked under the covers with Camellia snuggled tightly against his chest.

"For you, maybe," Camellia replied, running a hand up and down Henry's muscular arm.

"There have been a number of openings recently for radiologists around the country. It may not be New York, but–"

"Are you suggesting we *leave* New York?" Camellia's head popped up to look at her husband, her body tense all over again.

"We may not have a choice. I haven't had any promising leads around here. Neither have you."

"Thanks a lot." She sat up and wrapped the sheet around her, inching herself away from Henry.

"I didn't mean that as a snub," he said, feeling for her leg and getting a shot of uncharacteristic stubble. "I'm just being realistic. We're at the point where we have to go where the jobs are."

"And just where are the jobs?"

"I have an interview with a group in Michigan."

"Michigan!" she cried out. "We don't know anybody in Michigan. What's in Michigan?" She got up and sat at the bench at the end of the bed, mindlessly picking at a hangnail, her heart racing.

"Don't get excited, it's just an interview. But it is reassuring to know I have some possibilities." Henry sat up, the remaining sheet falling away to reveal his toned upper body that was already losing its tan from their summer holiday on the French Riviera.

"Well don't scare me like that," she scolded. "Me without a job in New York is bad enough. But no job in Michigan? Sitting in an apartment all day not knowing a soul while you're busy at work? Might as well shoot me now and get it over with."

Henry chuckled. "Nice to see you've still got a fire in your belly." He crawled across the bed and scooped her up, pulling her on top of him. "Now come back over here and show me just how hot you are."

A week later, Henry stood at the front door with a garment bag and overnight duffle in hand, waiting for his wife to kiss him goodbye. "Just remember, the sooner I go, the sooner I can come back," Henry called out.

Camellia appeared from around the corner, her mouth in a pout. "How will I get through the next two days without you? I fear I've become completely dependent on you."

"And you know I secretly love it." He set his bags down and took her in his arms. "It's just an interview and it's only two days." He kissed her forehead and each cheek. "Don't forget, we spent way more time apart when you were jetting off to fashion weeks around the world."

"Emphasis on *were*," Camellia said, pushing Henry away then pulling him back again to wrap her arms tightly around his neck. "Besides, I had plenty to do. There wasn't time to properly miss you."

"Well, see that, you can enjoy properly missing me for the next two days. Seriously, Camellia, why don't you call your mother?"

Camellia released Henry from her tight grip and sunk into the tufted chair set in the corner by the door. "My mother? Are you kidding me?"

"Do you have any idea how many times she's called the house since *Flair* folded? I don't, because I lost count."

"Har, har," she replied unconcerned, running a hand through what was now root-apparent hair.

"You haven't spoken with her once, Camellia. I, on the other hand, have experienced numerous conversations with Gina. Because I'm the only one who will talk to her. It's been three months, honey. And it's almost Christmas. If you asked her to, she would be here by dinnertime."

"Is that a threat, or a fact?"

"She's not a bad person, Camellia. You chose to run away from her lifestyle. You don't have to abandon her, too. He opened the door and picked up his bags. "I'll call you tonight."

Camellia closed the door softly behind him, wondering how she would pass the next two days alone. Calling Gina was out of the question. If her mother were to pick up on her depression, she really would be on a train and knocking down the door before Camellia could gather the strength to change out of her pajamas. Then, inspiration struck: a letter. A good, old-fashioned, thinking-about-you letter on good cardstock would satisfy Gina's need for information without a conversation. And it was significantly more thoughtful than a quick and easy email. She hurried to the office and pulled out her stack of stationery from the bureau. She had just enough time to write a few lines and still make the day's mail pickup.

The note card she selected had a red cover with her monogram stamped elegantly in white. With pen in hand, she stood over the desk, searching her mind for something appropriate to say that would be satisfying without saying too much. The mail carrier would be downstairs in minutes. The pressure made it all the more harder to focus. Finally, she started to write in her elegant, slanted script:

Mother,

Been terribly busy. As you can imagine, many offers have been presented to me, and trying to choose the one that is best for both Henry and me has been a challenge, to say the least. Sorry we'll be absent for Christmas. We hope by this time next year we are fully settled in our new roles and can enjoy the holidays in a leisurely manner. Give my love to Dad.

Yours,
Camellia

Scribbling the address on the envelope and licking it closed, Camellia threw on a long coat from the front closet, buttoning it to the top so her pajamas wouldn't show, and ran out the door to the elevator. By the time she made it to the ground floor, the mail carrier had already arrived and was chatting pleasantly with the concierge, whom Camellia had learned – after so many interactions sneaking in and out of the building – was named Mihail.

She scurried across the lobby, practically breathless by the time she reached the men. "I have mail," she announced, waving the envelope.

"I can take that," the mail carrier said, his thick mustache wiggling as he spoke.

"Thank you so much," Camellia replied softly, realizing this was the first conversation she had had with anyone outside her husband since Thanksgiving.

"Is there, um, anything else you need, Mrs. Rhodes?" Mihail said, looking at Camellia strangely.

Camellia followed his eyes down to her feet, which were bare. She blushed crimson. "Oh, no, no, I'm fine, Mihail, thank you. Just, uh, had an important letter to get out. Very important. All set now. Thanks again, gentlemen. Have a lovely afternoon."

She walked as quickly as she could back to the elevator, restraining the urge to break into a full run. Luckily the doors were still open and she clamored inside, holding her breath until the doors closed.

Once she was safely back in the apartment – she was shocked she hadn't managed to lock herself out in her rush – she threw the coat onto the tufted chair and went into her bedroom, pulling the covers off the bed and dragging them into the living room. She was tired of hiding out in her room. Now that Alain and Yara were gone, she could be a mess right out in the open.

After she threw the sheet and comforter over the sofa, she grabbed the remote and tossed that on top of the pile. Then she went into the kitchen, opening cabinets and scanning the shelves. Finding a silver tray, she placed on it an open bottle of Cabernet, a box of Carr's crackers, a thick chunk of Gruyére cheese, a container of chocolate ice cream, and a large spoon. She carried the teetering tray out to the living room, placing it on the square coffee table, then dragged the table so it was right beside the sofa. With everything in place, Camellia slipped under the covers, grabbed the remote, and powered on the flat-panel television. She reached for the bottle of wine and drank from it directly. It was dry and full, just how she liked it. Flipping mindlessly through the channels, she landed on MTV and smirked, barely recognizing the channel that in her youth had been fashion inspiration. Now it was filled with teenage dribble dressed in wife beaters and tattoos. She took another swig from the bottle and flipped the channel. Swig and flip. Swig and flip. Still on the tray, the ice cream sweated and melted and leaked.

When Henry arrived home two days later, Camellia was still on the couch. The covers haphazard over her body were covered in crumbs and food wrappers. And the silver tray now looked like a Jenga game, with containers and plastic wear stacked in a teetering heap. Henry's bright smile turned to an expression of concern. "Camellia, are you sick?"

Camellia pulled herself to a seated position and looked quizzically at her husband. "Uh, no, just camping out I guess," she replied groggily. She eyed Henry, who looked like he had just returned from a spa trip rather than a job interview. "Why do you look so fresh and wide-eyed?"

Pushing a pizza box onto the floor, Henry fit his body into the limited seating left on the sofa. He picked up his wife's legs and laid them across his knees, grimacing as he made contact with more pronounced leg hair, which didn't seem to phase Camellia. "First let me go on record that we're getting you into the shower today and cleaning your campsite."

"Whatever, funny man. Let's hear about your trip instead."

"It was terrific. The doctors in the group are as nice as can be and the offices are modern. They partner with two area hospitals and also do work for the outpatient-imaging center. There is an immediate need for a radiologist, too. Honey, we can be back in the black and living really well in no time."

"Whoa, whoa, whoa," Camellia said, ripping away the covers, the crumbs flying into the air then falling like rain. "Immediate need? Henry, what are you saying?"

"I'm saying they offered me a job, Camellia. We're moving to Michigan."

TEN

"I said, *what do you mean we're moving to Michigan?*" Camellia was close on Henry's heels as he carried his bags to their expansive walk-in closet. "You can't just go off and accept a job in another state without discussing it with me first."

"What would you have said? 'Oh Henry, what an amazing opportunity for us?'"

"No, because it isn't an amazing opportunity for *us*. It's an amazing opportunity for *you*."

"Is that so awful?" he roared. "For something great to happen to me? Wonderful things have been happening for you for years. And I've been your biggest cheerleader. No matter your moods or your single-minded decisions. Don't I get a turn?"

Camellia was speechless. Henry had never raised his voice to her in all their years together. And, much to her dismay, what he was saying held an awful lot of truth. Although that didn't make any of what was happening okay. If she were to leave New York, it would be like waving the white flag. She would be over in every conceivable way. Maybe if it were Los Angeles or Chicago, cosmopolitan cities with on-the-map Fashion Weeks and big publishing companies and flagship stores, the move could be seen as a strategic decision. But everyone in the fashion world would know there was nothing strategic about relocating to Michigan. They would know she had no other choice.

She began to weep, sinking onto the closet floor. "Henry, I don't think I can do this."

Henry stopped unpacking and stared at her. "What can't you do? Support your husband?"

"No, it's not that."

"Then what? You can't leave New York? They way I see it, neither of us have any options here at the moment."

"At the moment. It will get better. We'll find jobs."

"I found a job. With great pay and benefits."

"So maybe you can go and then once we get offers here, you can come back."

"You're suggesting we separate?" His voice was filled with vile.

"Not us. Not our marriage. Just for work. For a little while." She was sobbing. "Henry, *please*."

"None of those fashion people care one bit for you. They've made that perfectly clear. The only person supporting you is me. How dare you throw me away for them?" He threw the duffle bag to the floor and stomped out.

"Henry!" Camellia shrieked. She scrambled to her feet and chased after him, but it was too late. The front door slammed shut. He was gone.

Camellia paced the apartment, a sick swirl of anxiety, nausea, and exhaustion following her. Making tough decisions had always been one of her strongest assets. Now she felt paralyzed – unable to take a positive step in any direction. She stopped trying to find work a month ago, fully believing no one was going to consider her for a position, neither in fashion nor publishing in general. Even queries to smaller fitness and business magazines had come back empty. What was she going to do, fold sweaters at JCrew? So, instead she did nothing, watching the last of their savings drain away, while Henry punched away at the calculator, agonizing over the bills, and wondering how they would pay their costly apartment lease next month.

She found herself in the doorway of the office, and couldn't help but notice that her laptop was starting to collect dust. She wandered in and slumped into the desk chair, opening the lid of the computer. Safari was already running, its Google search box waiting for direction. She typed in "Michigan" and hit enter. A number of sites for the University of Michigan popped up, along with a Wikipedia listing. While she would have thwarted one of her editors for sourcing the sometimes-unreliable site, she clicked on the link, figuring she would get a simple-to-read picture of the state holding Henry's promise.

The entry noted that Michigan was the eighth most populated state in the country known for its lakes. While it wouldn't be the Amalfi Coast, living on the water could hold some promise. She read about the auto industry, which reminded her that she hadn't driven a car in nearly two decades. The fact that she couldn't find one word about mass transportation concerned her, however with Henry's salary, they could again afford car service. The state had a decent amount of tourism, although she couldn't be sure what vacationers were heading there to do. There were beautiful photos on the page, showing Tahquamenon Falls and Sleeping Bear Dunes and a charming spot called Mackinac Island. That gave her a glimmer of hope, until she read that the major industries included cars, cereal, and pizza. Still, she hadn't yet found what she was really searching for, so she Googled "Michigan shopping".

She reeled back as an all-Christmas-all-the-time shopping destination called Bronner's popped up on the search results, the overload of sparkly décor giving her an instant headache. Scrolling quickly down through the list, she landed on a site showcasing Michigan's best shops and malls, and there, amidst the scores of fudge shops and outdoor stores, she found real promise in the names of Neiman Marcus, Saks Fifth Avenue, Gucci, Louis Vuitton, and Salvatore Ferragamo. There were also listings for St. John and Stuart Weitzman and Ralph Lauren and Henri Bendel, too. Halleluiah. Michigan had shopping.

Getting up from the desk, she went back into the living room to look out at Central Park, the oasis adding to her growing sense of calm. She imagined a life in a sprawling Cape-Cod cottage with a dormered roof and a second-floor balcony overlooking the water. She pictured a quieter, yet cultured life, filled with gallery exhibits, foreign films, shopping excursions, and alfresco dining. While Camellia wasn't yet sure what she could do for work, she imagined she could set a course for greatness as a freelance writer, starting with some of the up-and-coming fashion websites, and slowly moving back into magazines, until once again she was being sent to cover fashion weeks and boutique openings all over the world. Yes, this was a life she could find enthusiasm for. A life she could share with Henry.

When Henry finally returned home later that evening, he found a different wife waiting for him. Camellia was showered and dressed in wide-legged trousers and a silk-print blouse, her hair sleek, and her makeup back in place. And most remarkable: she was smiling.

"Camellia?" he questioned, looking unsure of his wife's sudden change.

"Henry, let's do this," she said brightly. "Let's move to Michigan."

"What changed?" Henry asked, tearing into his steak. They had decided to go out for a celebratory dinner at a little restaurant around the corner from their apartment, followed by a small shopping trip to select Christmas gifts for each other.

It was the first time Camellia had been out in ages, and she couldn't deny how good it felt to be amongst people again, especially with no more threat of paparazzi following her. "I did some research," she explained, delicately stabbing at her Salade Niçoise. "I didn't realize how lovely Michigan is."

"It really is," Henry agreed. "I didn't get a chance to tell you earlier, but one of the group's receptionists, Mary Wysocki, has a friend who recently got transferred to Atlanta, and is looking to rent out his house until the real estate market improves. It's empty, and she says very picturesque, and it's ours to call home for awhile."

Camellia set her fork down. Her forehead was creased, but she was too concerned with this new information to remember about wrinkles. "You agreed to a house without me seeing it first?"

"Well, it's not like we have time to go house hunting. The director of the practice wants me to start as soon as possible. Besides, it's just a rental. Once we get our bearings, we can determine the neighborhood we like and find our own house to buy."

"We're buying a house?"

"Sure, why wouldn't we? It's a buyer's market, and we can use some equity."

Camellia looked down at her lap. "It just sounds so...permanent."

Henry reached across the table, taking his wife's hand into his own. "Honey, I'll make you a deal. If this move doesn't work out for us, we can come back to New York. Honest. We just have to promise that we'll give it a chance. Will you give it a chance?"

Camellia nodded, trying hard to remember that picture she had created of the grand house and the life of leisure. She could give it a chance. She would do it for Henry.

After dinner, they took a cab to Barneys on Madison Avenue. Camellia was delighted to be back in one of her favorite department stores, surrounded by luxurious designer goods and happy people with platinum cards at the ready. They parted at the front doors and Camellia stayed on the first floor, heading to men's accessories. She circled the sunglass cases, deciding that life on the water called for a very good pair of designer shades with proper UV protection. The slim, well-dressed salesman kindly extracted pair after pair, even consenting to model the different styles. She decided on a handsome aviator style by Tom Ford, experiencing only minor anxiety as the salesman placed the five-hundred-dollar order on her credit card.

Camellia found Henry in the jewelry department, accepting a small bag with ribbon poking out the top from an older saleslady with stunning white hair. When he noticed her standing there, he dramatically pretended to stash the bag inside his overcoat. "I knew you'd be here," she gushed. "I can smell a jewelry purchase from a mile away."

"Guilty," he said, putting an arm around his wife and escorting her to the door. "But you won't know exactly what it is until Christmas, smarty pants."

"Oh no, I have to wait *three whole days*. I think I can handle it."

Henry grinned. "I think you can handle a whole hell of a lot."

ELEVEN

Christmas arrived the way Camellia and Henry preferred, with a light snow falling on the city, and just the two of them at home, enjoying the magical quality of the morning. They sipped French-press coffee in front of the fireplace, the presents from Barney's set between them.

"I'm sorry I didn't get a tree this year," Camellia said, leaning into a leather ottoman.

"It's been a rough few months," Henry conceded. "You were hardly in the spirit, which is understandable."

Camellia watched the flames dancing behind the wrought-iron screen, and remembered this would be their last Christmas spent in the apartment. "I wonder if the house in Michigan has a fireplace."

"I don't know. I guess we'll find out soon enough." Henry pushed a present wrapped in thick striped paper to Camellia. "Why don't you open your present?"

She set her cup and saucer on the stone floor in front of the fireplace, and handed Henry his present. "No, you first," she commanded.

Henry smiled, turning the rectangular package in his hands. "I can't imagine what it could be."

"Then I guess you better open it."

He tore the paper and lifted the lid of the box. "Sunglasses?"

"Not just any sunglasses," she replied, cracking open the lid of the case.

"Oh, nice choice," Henry said, lifting the glasses and admiring the design.

"I figured a life on the water required serious shades," she explained proudly.

"A life on the water?"

"Have you any idea how many lakes there are in Michigan?"

Henry tried on the sunglasses, modeling them for Camellia. "Somebody's been doing her homework. Are we going to become sailors, then?"

Camellia thought about that for a minute. How decadent it would be to have their own sailboat, taking little voyages together and making friends with glorious yacht owners. "Maybe we shall," she said, nodding her approval.

"I'm so glad you're getting excited about the move. The truck will be here on the second, so we're going to need some excitement in our blood to get this apartment packed up in time."

Camellia's expression turned serious. "Aren't we hiring movers?"

"Yes, but we still have to be careful with our finances for awhile, and we already agreed to be a little indulgent with Christmas presents.

According to our lease, we have to keep paying for the apartment for three more months, and I won't start getting paid immediately. So we have to box up our own stuff. The movers will get everything into and out of the truck.

"Fun."

"Ah, it will keep us occupied," Henry said, pushing the sunglasses onto his head.

"Will it ever."

"Okay, Mrs. Sarcasm, let's settle you down with a present, shall we?"

Eyes wide, Camellia reached for her present, delicately pulling at the tape. Keeping the paper perfectly intact, she slid it away, revealing a pretty red case. She raised her eyebrows at Henry then opened the lid, revealing a gleaming solid-gold bracelet with a heart attached to it.

"It's a charm bracelet," Henry explained, lifting it from the case and attaching it to her outstretched wrist. "The heart represents my love for you. As we venture into this new chapter of our lives, I'll add charms to the bracelet that represent all the good things we find along the way."

"Henry," Camellia said softly, her eyes filled with tears. "You are the sweetest man I have ever known." She pressed her weight into him, kissing him deeply. He pulled her on top of him and ran his hands down her backside, pressing her against his erection. Within seconds, he had her undressed and pinned beneath him on the plush rug. She giggled from the tickle of the rug against her bare skin, and spread her legs to welcome Henry inside her, which was as warm and inviting as the dancing fire.

They spent the week between Christmas and New Year's taping together boxes Henry had ordered from the moving company and thoughtfully placing their lives into them. They split up the duties, with Henry focusing on the kitchen, and Camellia dealing with their master closet and bathroom. Before tackling the closet, Camellia perched on one of the oversized leather cubes positioned in the center of the space and surveyed her collection.

The closet was a fashion-lover's dream, with floor-to-ceiling white cabinetry, soft shelf lighting, and a dazzling chandelier. Her collection was well edited: classic suiting and day dresses mixed with eye-catching cocktail wear and couture gowns. And then there were the bags and shoes. Every style, by every major designer, in every color was lined up in perfect rows for easy viewing. Henry's section was just as impressive, with numerous suits, trousers, and button-downs hanging perfectly over two rows of shining shoes; his T-shirts and sweaters folded neatly in a tall shelving unit. Even though she had spent years getting dressed in this closet, it still took her breath away each time she turned on the light and stepped inside.

She sighed and dragged in a large packing box, grateful Henry had thought to order wardrobe boxes so she could leave the majority of her clothing on hangers, saving her hours of folding and steaming time. Only her sweaters, lingerie, and accessories would need to go into regular boxes.

Twenty-four wardrobe boxes later, the hanging section of the closet was packed, save for a grouping of outfits she had set aside for Henry and her to wear during their last days in the apartment. Already exhausted, she retied the silk scarf that was covering her hair and wandered toward the kitchen to check on Henry's progress. She found him in the living room, reclining on the sofa with a glass of beer in hand and the Giants game on the television. "Slacking off, I see?"

"Done, my dear. How about you?"

"You're *done*? With the whole kitchen? How is that possible?"

Henry took a long drink of his beer and looked at his wife quizzically. "It's been five hours," he said, his eyes never straying from the game. "And those kitchen boxes were fantastic. Little spots for the glasses to go so they don't have to be wrapped. Same for the plates. Really made it simple. Yes! First down."

With Henry's full attention back on the game, Camellia headed to the kitchen to see for herself. Sure enough, the cabinets were bare, and boxes were stacked everywhere, with only a narrow path to the refrigerator left open. She opened the refrigerator, feeling famished, and pulled out a couple of cheese hunks and went into the pantry for some crackers. They were packed. She opened the silverware drawer for a knife. That was packed. Every last plate was packed, too. And there were no paper goods to be found. With a noisy exhale, she threw the cheese back into the refrigerator and headed back to the closet. "Real thorough packing job, Henry," she muttered as she passed through the living room, Henry too focused on the football game to respond.

By moving day they were done and barely able to put one leg in front of the other, their bodies aching from all the bending and lifting. Henry had rented an SUV for them to drive, which was packed with more urgent personal belongings, including Camellia's laptop and a bag filled with toiletries, just in case the moving truck broke down en route. Henry planned to keep the car for a week, until he could buy them their own. Camellia hoped Henry also planned on taking care of all the driving. A road trip was not the right time to revisit the lessons learned in driver's education.

It took the movers until early afternoon to get all the boxes and furniture out of the apartment. Henry had positioned himself outside near the back of the truck, making sure their possessions made it safely onto the vehicle. Camellia, however, didn't know what to do with herself. The movers didn't require any direction, the four young, able-bodied men huffing in and out of the apartment, careful not to nick the walls as they maneuvered bulky tables and dressers and chairs out the door with ease. As the day progressed, there were less places to sit, and no place to escape. Finally, she took the elevator down to wait with Henry. When the door opened at the lobby, Tray was waiting.

"Cammie!" he shrieked with mock joy, taking in her simple road-trip outfit of tailored Capri pants, cashmere sweater, and ballet flats. "Don't tell me you're leaving us."

"If you'll excuse me, Tray, I'm busy," she replied gruffly. She tried to pass by, but he blocked her way.

"What's the matter, Cammie? No one in New York wants to hire you?"

Camellia felt her blood pressure rise. She wondered if she were to hit him square in the jaw, what he could possibly do to harm her more than he already had. An assault charge would be the least of her worries. "Get out of my way," she seethed, "or I'll scream."

Tray doubled over with fits of laughter, slapping his leg overdramatically. "That's rich," he crowed, and then leaned in close. "That's the only thing rich about you, though, isn't it? An overpaid editor-in-chief who doesn't listen to her boss learns just how quickly the money runs out, doesn't she?"

Camellia let out a long, high-pitched scream that sent Tray tumbling into the elevator and a handful of building staff running in her direction. "Are you okay, Miss?" the doorman asked, whipping out a cell phone from his jacket pocket to call for help.

Camellia nodded, and turned to Tray, who looked like a deer in headlights at the very back of the still-open elevator, Camellia's foot strategically holding the door in check. "I always do what I say I will," she said, her voice a mixture of pluck and loathing. "And mark my words, darling Tray: My comeback will make you regret the day you tossed aside Camellia Rhodes." She excised her foot from the elevator door, and watched with pleasure as Tray Mathers disappeared from view.

TWELVE

"You actually said 'Mark my words?' Damn, I can't believe I missed it!" Henry proclaimed, as he navigated the Manhattan traffic en route to the Lincoln Tunnel.

Camellia sat beside him in the rented Range Rover, beaming over both her performance and Henry's enthusiastic approval. "You should have seen his face," she mused. "If he could have pushed his way through the steel wall of that elevator, he would have."

Henry patted her hand. "You always did know how to make an exit."

The plan was to take Interstate 80 across Pennsylvania and Ohio, then head north on 75 to reach their destination in Michigan. It would take about fourteen hours, including stops for food and to stretch their legs. The moving van was scheduled to arrive the following morning. Henry had picked up an air mattress and packed pillows and blankets so they could get a few hours of sleep before unpacking began.

The journey was more fun than Camellia had expected. She hadn't been on a road trip since she went with her parents to the Poconos for a long weekend camping trip the day after graduating from high school. It was their idea of a graduation present: cramped sleeping in a too-small tent with fishing and hiking the daily activities. It was her worst nightmare, complete with swarms of mosquitoes and a mild case of poison ivy. For Camellia, it was proof positive her parents didn't understand her at all.

Now with Henry, the mood was light, in a luxurious vehicle with old '80s songs on the satellite radio, and a venti cappuccino in her hands. Snow covered the Pennsylvania mountains, but the roads were clear, making the drive as beautiful as it was peaceful.

They stopped for a late dinner north of Pittsburgh at a charming café with lace curtains and a stocked pie rack. Camellia ordered a big leafy salad so she wouldn't feel too guilty about the slice of key lime pie she was eyeing.

"We're not going to get in until around four in the morning, so you might want to nap once we're back in the car," Henry suggested, pouring a pitcher of gravy over an oversized pile of homemade mashed potatoes. Camellia shook her head. "You don't want to sleep?" he asked.

"No, I don't understand how you can eat like that and never gain a pound," she muttered, stabbing at a spinach leaf.

"Good genes," he replied, lifting a forkful of potatoes to his mouth. "Can you imagine, with my ability to stay slim and your ability to always look fabulous, how gorgeous our baby will be?"

"Oh Henry, are you pregnant?" Camellia questioned. "You won't be skinny for long."

"Come on, you have to admit, we've got some good DNA between us."

Camellia set down her fork and crossed her arms. "You don't think for one minute, now that you got me out of New York, that I'm going to transform into your little stay-at-home baby-making machine, do you?"

"Of course not. But damn, Camellia, we've been married for eight years. Isn't it about time?"

She sighed. It wasn't that she didn't like babies, or that she was completely opposed to the idea. They probably would have beautiful children. And Henry would make a wonderful father, she had no doubt. But when it came to picturing herself as a mother, Camellia got cold feet. Her own mother had been devoted to her and yet had zero idea who Camellia was – not then or now. How would she do with her own child? And then there was the issue of her career, or more appropriate, her need to build a new career. Now that she was back at the bottom again, with a looming climb in front of her, how would a child figure into her plans to fight her way back to the top? And once she was traveling to fashion weeks and fundraising galas again, who would look after the baby? Henry's job would be keeping him busy, leaving their baby in the care of a nanny. How would she feel about someone else raising her child? She couldn't help but feel paralyzed by the thought of fitting a baby into her world.

"I'll think about it, okay?" she finally said. Henry flashed her a look that made her realize her husband no longer believed her when it came to this subject. "I promise," she reaffirmed. "I really will think about it."

Camellia pushed the leafy salad about her plate with her fork, her chest heavy as her mind pushed around a lingering thought she couldn't shake.

"What is it?" Henry's eyes were concerned.

She set down her fork and put her hands in her lap. Her eyes were downcast. "Henry, why do you put up with me?"

"Because I love you," Henry replied without missing a beat.

Camellia looked up at him. "That's a little simplistic, don't you think? I'm a workaholic who spends money like water and expects everyone to do what I want, including you. I've set aside your requests to start a family again and again and again." Her expression was pained, her eyebrows knit tight. "How can anyone love a person like that?"

Henry wiped his mouth on his napkin and folded his arms on the table. His expression, surprisingly, was one of amusement. "If you're asking me if you drive me crazy, the answer is a resounding yes."

Camellia's mouth dropped open at her husband's frankness. "Henry, I–"

"Let me finish," he interrupted.

Camellia fell silent, her eyes once again staring into her lap.

"You are a strong, fiercely independent woman who knows what she wants. I knew that from the moment I met you. That's exciting. Challenging, too. Compromise isn't easy with you." Camellia crossed her arms as Henry continued. "Over the years you've had to build a tough shell around you to protect you from the negativity that comes from having such a high-level, highly public job. I get that. However, at some point, you stopped remembering that you don't need that shell protecting you from your personal life. But none of this changes my love for you. You're the one I've always wanted, Camellia. You may drive me crazy, but there's no one I'd rather have doing it."

"I've been a real shithead," she said as two tears slid down her cheeks. She brushed them away while blinking back the brigade still threatening to fall. "Henry." She inhaled deeply and closed her eyes, as if preparing to leap from a cliff. "I have to tell you something that I did. Or almost did."

"What is it?"

She grabbed her napkin and held it at her face, hiding the majority of it from sight. "I was going to fire an emotionally unstable girl who had been doing a good job to make a point." Her breath hitched as the memory resurfaced. The tears flowed. "It would have been the absolute lowest thing I had ever done. And I was practically reveling in it."

"But you said 'almost did.'"

"Yeah. Funny enough, Tray fired me first."

"Oh. I see."

"I understand protecting myself, but I don't know how I became this person." Camellia dabbed at her face then set down the napkin, revealing blotchy skin and puffy eyes. "I don't like me."

"Well you can't de-shithead yourself overnight," Henry said, picking up a leftover menu from the table, a smile playing on his lips, "so don't worry too much. You'll find yourself again. Now how about that dessert?"

Two hearty slices of pie and two steaming cups of coffee later, they were back on the road. Though Camellia didn't think she would be able to sleep, she drifted off easily, the sound of the tires on the road like a one-note lullaby. She woke to dim light coming in through the tinted windows, surprised to find it was already early morning. Hitting the lever to raise the seat back, she turned to Henry, who was winding his way along a two-lane road that was flanked by massive fir trees. "Are you okay?"

"Tired," Henry said, his hands tight on the wheel.

She looked at the little clock on the dash. It was just after five a.m. "Have you been driving all night?"

"I took a little break just after crossing the Michigan border. Stopped for a coffee and some snacks at a truck stop."

"Oh honey," she said, reaching over to rub Henry's neck. "I'm sorry I slept so long."

"It's okay. You're in charge of telling the movers where to put everything, so you're going to need to be thinking straight."

He made a sharp turn onto a quiet road with little wooden houses spread far apart, surrounded by large plots of land. "Where are we?" Camellia asked, running a hand through her hair.

"We're here." Henry made a right into a gravel driveway, reminiscent of the one at his parent's place. But the little wooden structure overshadowed by giant trees that was aglow from the SUV's headlights was a far cry from Carl and Lena's quaint getaway.

"This isn't a house, it's barely a cottage," Camellia said, alarmed. "Please tell me this is a mistake."

"Don't worry," Henry said, already out of the car, shaking out his legs. "It's rather cute. And I'm sure it's great inside." He walked up to the door and bent down to pull a set of keys out from under the welcome mat.

"People really do that here?" she scoffed, as Henry dangled the keys at her.

"Come on, let's go in," he called out.

"It's five o'clock in the morning, keep your voice down," she reprimanded, trudging up the path to the door.

"I don't think anyone could hear me if I screamed," he said, motioning around at the lack of neighbors.

"That's comforting," she mumbled, stepping past the screen door Henry was holding open. She felt for the light to the right of the door and flicked it on. Her Valentino handbag fell to the linoleum floor.

In front of her were the main rooms of the house: a living room, kitchen, and dining area, and they were already furnished. The living room featured a matching oversized sofa and chair in country blue and tiny white flowers, with the same blue used for the carpet and valences. A wooden coat rack, floor lamp, and an old TV pushed into the corner all surrounded what appeared to be the room's centerpiece – a wood-burning stove with an ugly pipe that traveled up and out the wall behind it.

The dining area had the same carpet and valences, with a black rectangular table and six simple round-back chairs. A large pendant light hung over the table about ten feet in the air, dangling from the pitched ceiling.

The kitchen was very small, with a refrigerator and stove at one end, a peninsula with two barstools at the other end, and a counter with a sink and cabinets above and below connecting both ends. A little microwave sat on the counter. There was no dishwasher. The wall over the stove was decorated with ducks and fish and a square clock.

All three rooms were painted the same salmon color and had stained oak trim around the windows and up the narrow stairway to what Camellia assumed were the bedrooms. She hadn't yet seen a bathroom, and was concerned it could be located outside.

"This can't be the right house," she said, still hopeful Henry had gotten the address wrong.

"I'm afraid it is." Henry set the keys on a ledge beside the door. "Come on, let's see where we're going to be sleeping." They climbed the stairs to find a single, cramped bedroom, just large enough to fit a double bed, two narrow nightstands, and a little wooden dresser. The bedspread was a patchwork quilt with bears, leaves, and cabins surrounded by a border of diamond-shape patches in a palette of beige, brown, and hunter green. "It's a back-country bedroom," Henry said, his voice too tired to be sarcastic.

Off the bedroom was the only bathroom, one of the more roomy areas of the house, with toilet, sink, a free-standing vanity with built-in mirror, and a shower stall. "Oh my God, there's no tub," Camellia realized.

"There's probably a rain barrel in the yard you can soak in."

"Henry, that's not funny. We can't live here."

"We're going to have to, for a little while." He squeezed past Camellia to get from the bathroom back to the top of the stairs. "I'll grab our bags. For now, we need to get some sleep. The movers will be here in a few hours."

"They won't have much to do, will they?" she muttered, going back into the bedroom and flinging herself on the bed. The old mattress springs bounced her up and down, squeaking as they went. "Oh good God."

Henry reappeared with their overnight bags in hand, which he tucked on either side of the dresser. He stripped down to his boxers, dug in his bag for his toiletries kit, and trudged into the bathroom. "We have water," he announced, the thunderous sound of the groaning pipes that carried the water to the second floor negating explanation.

Sliding into bed, Henry kissed his wife on the cheek and turned back to extinguish the ceramic lamp on his nightstand. Within minutes, he was snoring. Camellia, however, was unable to sleep. The long nap in the SUV mixed with the surreal surroundings of this ramshackle cottage kept her eyes peeled open, her mind whirling with alternative housing options. They could easily tuck the keys back under the doormat and check into a nearby hotel. At least they would have a bed that didn't sound like it was rescued from her great-grandmother's attic, and a restaurant where she could have her meals when she didn't feel like ordering room service. She could also hire a real estate agent first thing in the morning, and find the type of well-appointed home on the water she had anticipated. Better yet, they could do both – move to a hotel in the morning and be out scouting properties by afternoon. With a plan of action settled on, Camellia finally drifted into slumber, only to be awakened three hours later by a pounding on the front door. The movers had arrived.

Henry wasn't budging from his deep sleep, so she slithered out of bed, still fully dressed from the drive, and stumbled downstairs, opening the door to bright light and two burly moving men standing in the front yard smoking cigarettes.

"We have a bit of a problem," she called out, shielding her eyes from the sun that was reflecting off the snow. "Place is furnished and it's way too small to hold our things. Everything needs to go into storage."

One of the guys with a blue bandana tied around his head nodded and flicked the butt of his cigarette into the street. Camellia shook her head and closed the door on them, heading into the kitchen to look for a phone book. She found it in the cupboard under the sink, damp with curling pages. Disgusted, she placed the thin book on the counter and flipped through the Yellow Pages to the entries for storage units. There was one listing for a place called U Store Stuff. She realized she had absolutely no idea where it was in relation to the cottage. In fact, she had no idea what city the cottage was in. "Where the hell am I?" she wondered aloud. She climbed the stairs again and burst into the bedroom. "Henry, what city is this?"

Henry rolled over, his groaning mostly drowned out by the rattling mattress springs. He sat up and looked around, his expression dazed. "Are the movers here?"

"Yes, and we need a storage unit fast. I have no idea where we are to judge the distance of the storage facility."

"Markleeville," he said, yawning and scratching at his back.

"Seriously?" Camellia questioned, glaring at him. "You moved me to a place called Markleeville?" She laughed out loud. "That's just fabulous." She plodded back down the stairs to call the storage unit. "Fab-u-lous!" she cried, her shrill voice ringing through the tiny house.

U Store Stuff was only two miles away. Henry and Camellia got back into the Range Rover and led the way, the moving truck laboring behind. To get to the storage unit, Henry had to drive north along Beech Street through downtown Markleeville, a sleepy town with a storybook quality, especially covered in a layer of snow. The sidewalks were empty of pedestrians, and only a handful of cars were parallel parked along the main thoroughfare. The buildings held a hodgepodge of services, with a post office, pharmacy, hardware store, and real estate office anchoring the ends of the diminutive downtown. Interspersed were a toy store, candy store, ice cream parlor, bakery, bait shop, bookstore, frame shop, and a narrow business offering backyard décor. There was a barbershop and salon sitting side-by-side, with a pizzeria and a diner bookending them. On opposite sides of the street were two women's boutiques. From the looks of their front windows, they were sharing an inventory of crew-neck sweaters and tapered trousers.

Just up the road, a car wash, animal hospital, and church were clustered together, as if they had seceded from the downtown. From there to the storage unit, they passed two more churches, a party store, a run-down motel, a hidden campground, two trailer parks, a seasonal farmers market, a boat and kayak rental company, a cemetery, and an equipment rental business. The intersection of Beech and Mitchell, where the storage unit was located, was also the site of the US-127 on- and off-ramp; a busier area with a Save-a-Lot, Dollar General, gas station/Taco Bell combo, movie theater, Econo Lodge, and fast-food row of McDonalds, Burger King, and Arby's.

Camellia was speechless.

At the storage unit, she and Henry sorted through boxes, their fingertips turning white from the cold as they searched for clothing, kitchen supplies, and any other easy-to-grab comforts from home to take back to the cottage. Everything else went into neat towers in the ten-by-twenty-five-foot unit. Henry signed papers with both the movers and the storage facility manager, and then locked the unit, adding the key to the rental car keychain that also held the cottage key.

"Want to get some coffee?" Henry asked, unzipping his jacket once he was back in the car.

"Absolutely," Camellia replied, rubbing her hands together for warmth.

They drove back into town, parking in front of the Beech Street Diner. Henry held the door to the diner for his wife, a tinny bell announcing them. The diner, painted pink and green, was large enough to hold ten tables plus the L-shaped counter with stools bolted to the tan and white checkerboard floor. The only other customers were two middle-age men with considerable bellies, wearing navy work pants and rugged brown jackets. A stout, dark-skinned woman behind the counter made coffee. On the radio, which was sitting on the end of the counter, a weepy country singer with a deep, twangy voice sang about a lost love.

Henry and Camellia sat at the short side of the counter near the door. The waitress, named Irene, according to the tag on her apron, set two cups down in front of them and poured coffee without asking. "You folks lost?" she asked, her voice loud enough to address the entire restaurant, had there been more than four customers present.

"Just moved to town last night, actually," Henry explained, clutching the warm cup in his hands.

Irene eyed them both in disbelief. "You two...moved here? What, are you in the Witness Protection Program or something?"

Henry laughed. "No. I took a job with a radiology practice a few miles away."

Irene set the coffee pot on the counter and leaned on her elbows, engrossed. "Oh, a doctor! My papa always wanted me to marry a doctor," she said with a note of disdain to Camellia. "Instead, I married a carpenter with a tendency to fall off of things. He's currently at home nursing a broken collarbone."

Camellia gave the waitress a weak smile and drank her equally weak coffee. Irene frowned and turned her attention back to Henry.

"You at Northern Medical Center?"

"Yes, and Mercy, too. There's also supposed to be an imaging center around here, right?"

"Yep, I see that place when I get up to Walmart. It's right next-door."

"Get up to Walmart?" Camellia piped in.

"Oh yeah, it's a bit of a drive, four miles I'd say, but it's worth knocking out a little gas in my tank. They have *everything* at Walmart."

Camellia groaned, slipped on her coat, and grabbed the keys from the counter. "I have to make a phone call," she lied. "I'll be in the car."

Irene huffed and refilled Henry's cup. "What's her problem?"

"My wife just needs a little time to adjust. It's a big change from New York to Markleeville."

"New York to *Markleeville?*" Irene screeched. "That's like going from a Ferrari to a Model T. Your wife's gonna need a whole load of time to get used to this place."

THIRTEEN

Two days after arriving in Markleeville, Henry started his new job with a meeting at the radiology practice's office, located across the street from Northern Medical Center, just a mile and a half west of Markleeville. It was Camellia's first time alone in the cottage, and she was determined to keep busy.

It had been years since she had cleaned up anything more than her own breakfast dishes, but the cottage had been sitting unused for some time, and had acquired a thick layer of dust. She searched the kitchen cabinets as well as the shelves in the tiny mudroom that joined the house to the garage, and came up empty. The best she could find in the garage was a half-used roll of paper towel. She would have to walk to town. Pulling her tall Gucci boots over black skinny denim, she threw on her short fur coat and a pair of cropped leather gloves and exited the front door, locking it behind her. The cottage was only three blocks from town, but with a cutting, bitter wind hitting her exposed ears, the trek felt like miles.

The town was just as eerily quiet as it was the morning she and

Henry had driven through en route to the storage facility. Only a few cars dotted the street and she was the only soul on foot. As she looked in the store windows, trudging along the single block that made up the heart of the downtown, Camellia realized she had limited choices for cleaning supplies. Limited choices for everything, really. Each store had a monopoly on the goods they were selling, save for the two women's boutiques that only differentiated themselves by their names. On the same side of the street as the diner was Lisa's Designs, and directly across the road was Cozy Corner. They both looked and sounded hopelessly outdated.

Toward the end of the block was a hardware store plainly called Henry's Hardware, and Camellia stepped inside, grateful for the blast of heat that greeted her, along with the same tinkling bell as the diner's. Inside was aisle upon aisle of this and that, from placemats to power tools, with a rectangular counter in the center with a cash register and unmissable display for key making. This appeared to be the only source in town willing to wedge any and all household needs into one, overcrowded space.

"Can I help you ma'am?" The boy behind the counter was young and somewhat handsome, with freshly buzzed dark hair and strong features. He was staring at her beyond that of friendly customer service.

"I'm okay, but thanks," Camellia said, making a legitimate attempt to be friendly. Then, noticing the boy was still gawking at her, her attitude turned defensive. "Anything wrong?" she questioned, with an air of authority.

The boy broke out into a wide, toothy grin. "Oh, no ma'am. I just never seen anyone dressed like you before."

Camellia wasn't sure if the boy's declaration was a compliment or mere observation. "What's your name?" she demanded.

"Caleb, ma'am."

"Caleb, do you think you could point me in the direction of cleaning supplies?"

"Sure. Aisle seven, ma'am."

"Caleb?"

"Yes ma'am?"

"You're going to have to stop calling me ma'am. You're aging me by the minute."

"Sorry ma'am!" Caleb called as Camellia strutted over to cleaning supplies, shaking her head.

She grabbed a bottle of Windex, a can of cleanser, another roll of paper towel, and a heavy-duty sponge, and carted them back to the counter. Caleb rang up her purchases and placed them in a paper bag. "Seven dollars and fifty seven cents," he announced, looking pleased for ending a sentence without the unwanted ma'am attached. Camellia pulled out her Visa and handed it to Caleb. "Ten dollar limit on credit cards, ma'am."

"Seriously?"

"I know. Sorry about the ma'am thing. I can't help it. My grandma would strike me down if I was disrespectful to a lady."

"No, I mean, you seriously can't take my credit card?" Camellia tapped her foot impatiently.

"Oh sure I can. You just have to get to ten dollars."

Camellia huffed. "Fine." She scanned the contents of the store, noticing a couple of coffee makers on an endcap display. "I take it there aren't any Starbucks nearby."

"There's one in Traverse City," Caleb offered.

"Where's that?"

"'Bout ninety minutes away."

"I'll take the coffee maker."

Camellia lugged the bulky coffee-maker box and the bag of supplies the three blocks back to the cottage through the same cutting wind, wondering how hard it was going to be to find coffee beans.

Henry returned home just before six to find Camellia engulfed in the oversized chair, wrapped in her favorite cashmere throw, squinting at the local news on the TV that was coming in as snowy as the weather. "What's with the TV?" he asked.

"No cable," she muttered. "No internet access either."

"That won't do," he commiserated, taking off his jacket and hanging it on the coat rack. "Can you take care of that tomorrow?"

Camellia exhaled loudly. "Sure honey. What else do I have to do?"

Henry knelt in front of his wife. "I know this isn't what you were expecting. It wasn't what I was expecting either." He looked at the country décor surrounding them. "This place is temporary. We'll find a home we love."

"Henry, we could live in a mansion with a full staff. It would still be Markleeville. How am I supposed to survive here? There's no shopping, no Starbucks. Hell, there's barely any people!"

"Yes, actually, I found out about the lack of people."

"What? Where is everybody?"

"According to one of the partners, Markleeville isn't very populated until the weather turns warm. Then it explodes. Lots of tourists come for life on the lake and the small-town charm."

"And in the winter, it's a ghost town."

Henry nodded. "Afraid so. A large amount of summer homes here, apparently."

"Any chance that come summer this place will transform into the Hamptons?"

Henry kissed his wife's hands. "I'm kind of doubting it."

He headed upstairs to change with Camellia on his heels. "I'm surprised you have enough patients to keep you busy at one hospital, much less two of them."

"That's the thing," Henry noted, unbuttoning his shirt and slipping into a soft blue sweater. "With the amount of hunting, ice fishing, and skiing around the area, the hospitals can barely keep up. Northern Medical Center, which I saw today, isn't the kind of hospital we're used to. Very small scale. Barely enough staff to handle all the injuries and frost bite, not to mention every other reason people require medical care."

"So your practice will never need for patients."

"Nope. And I'll tell you another thing I learned. Around here, when a guy comes in with a gunshot wound, it's not going to be because of a burglary or some other act of violence. The poor fool most likely was mistaken for a deer."

"I'll keep that in mind," Camellia said, looking out the bedroom window at the thick woods that was their backyard, and thinking about how close hunters might get to the cottage. In Pennsylvania, the start of deer season was like a holiday, with many schools closing for the day so kids could go off with their fathers into the woods, rifles in hand. Camellia wondered how she allowed herself to come full circle to the very type of place she spent years trying to escape.

By the end of the week, Camellia had cable television and high-speed Internet. The second she had the installer out of the house, who was noticeably perplexed by her turban and lace bed jacket, she was back in the all-consuming country-blue chair, with laptop on lap, pulling up her Internet bookmarks for Style.com, The Cut on New York Magazine's site, and of course, Women's Wear Daily. She read everything she could find: new designer collaborations, hits and misses from movie premieres, trend forecasts, and all the buzz for Mercedes Benz Fashion Week, which was only a month away. For the first time in a decade she would not be attending the shows.

When Henry clumped into the cottage just past seven, the new snow heavy on his boots, Camellia was still in front of the laptop, which now had two extension cords tethering it to the power source on the other side of the room. Her turban and bed jacket were still in place.

Henry discovered his wife in this same arrangement each evening for the next two weeks, save for his days off, when he insisted Camellia put away the laptop and go on driving excursions to nearby towns. He even drove her as far as Traverse City, an hour-and-a-half drive along winding two-lane roads, hoping to lift her spirits with good shopping and a busier environment. However, Camellia was not impressed when they set foot in the Grand Traverse Mall, causing Henry to announce that there would be no more trips without a little online research.

"At least it's a full-fledged mall," he offered.

"Yes, with full-fledged mall *stores*," she reminded.

He interlaced his fingers in hers as they passed the typical store offerings of Express, Victoria's Secret, and Charlotte Russe. "Maybe we should lower our expectations," he said, gazing at the windows filled with cookie-cutter clothing.

"Maybe we should start online shopping."

"At least there's a real coffee shop," Henry said, pointing ahead. "I've seen what a good cappuccino can do for you. Let's go."

One full hour of coffee sipping and people watching was all Camellia could take. "Why do I feel like I'm the one people are watching?" she questioned as they sat at a little table with a wide view of the mall's second floor. The passersby of young families and teens traveling in groups, all in nondescript clothing topped with bulky outerwear, conspicuously gaped at Camellia's bright abstract dress and thigh-high boots.

"Well, you don't exactly blend in."

"These are Etro boots straight off the runway!" she exclaimed. "They are the epitome of chic!"

"I'm not disagreeing with you," Henry said, admiring Camellia's shapely legs covered in laced-up leather. "But I don't think the locals are used to seeing such grand fashion statements."

"Well, why the hell not?" Camellia questioned, getting up from the table and tossing her paper cup into the wastebasket. "Is exciting fashion only allowed in highly populated areas? Henry, it's not like there's no money around here. We're standing in the middle of a resort town and the only label people seem to understand is North Face."

They scurried through the frigid parking lot into the black Jeep Grand Cherokee Henry had purchased from an area dealer. "Why don't you drive?" Henry asked. "You've got to relearn sooner or later."

"Later please," Camellia said sharply, fastening the seatbelt.

"Don't you want your own car? To be able to take off whenever you like?"

Camellia looked at Henry and grinned devilishly. "Aren't you concerned I might start driving and not stop?"

He hit the gas and backed out of the parking spot. "Maybe I should be."

"I'll make you a deal: Once this ice melts and I don't have to worry that one bad turn will send me over an embankment, I'll give driving a try. But if I'm not comfortable, you're getting me a car and driver."

"In Markleeville?" Henry crowed. "That won't have people staring at you *at all*."

"Henry," Camellia sighed, gazing out at the quiet road in front of them, "Markleeville needs a serious makeover."

"And there's no one better to make that happen than you."

FOURTEEN

Camellia spent the first week of February glued to her laptop, ingesting any and all news she could search out on New York Fashion Week. The palette for Fall 2009 was noticeably somber, a telling sign of the troubled financial times. The clothing had a more timeless feel, not as frivolous as in years past, pointing to designers anticipating a woman's desire to fully utilize her wardrobe instead of chucking costly pieces to the curb the second a one-season trend's moment had passed. While Camellia didn't like why the movement was happening, she did approve of the end result.

She was also pleased her upper body was as toned as it was, with one-shoulder dresses and tunics showing up in most every collection from Carolina Herrera to Oscar de la Renta. However, she shuddered as she browsed far too many examples of an '80s revival for fall – especially from her beloved Marc Jacobs – complete with neon hues, tapered pants, and raised shoulders.

By the end of the week, Camellia knew without a doubt that she had to peel herself away from the computer and find something satisfying to do. She had spent days watching others' outstanding accomplishments sashay down runways while she was merely a bystander. While it was one thing to be invited to the shows, it was certainly another to silently watch from afar. She no longer contributed to anything. And it had to stop. Somehow, she had to find direction and the only place to look for it at the moment was Markleeville.

Still without a car or the will to drive, Camellia trekked back to town on foot, this time pairing a matching fur hat to her sumptuous fur jacket, and pleasantly discovering that warm ears made for a more bearable commute. As she walked she pledged not to leave the town until she found one single thing that interested her. She also added in a pledge to first stop for a steaming cup of coffee. Her interest was piqued the moment she walked into the diner.

Behind the counter was a tall, willowy girl with long dark blonde hair dressed in black jeans and a slouchy black t-shirt. She looked positively chic and effortless at the same time. As she poured coffee for a couple at the counter, Camellia observed the girl's high cheekbones and full lips. If this were New York, a modeling agent would have walked into this joint, taken one look at that girl, and had her signed before the day was over. But this was Markleeville. That girl could rot here and no one would ever understand what she had to offer.

A loud crash tore Camellia from her thoughts, and as she refocused, she realized the girl had dropped the coffee pot and was staring directly at her, her mouth agape. "Are you okay?" Camellia asked approaching the counter, concerned the girl might have had a seizure.

"Oh my God. You're Camellia *Rhodes*," the girl gushed, bordering on hyperventilation.

Camellia felt dizzy upon hearing her name. She couldn't believe someone had recognized her in Markleeville. She wanted to throw her arms around the girl, but reminded herself about constraint and instead held out her hand. "I am," she said, perfectly poised. "How do you do?"

The girl squealed and grabbed Camellia's hand like it was a lifeline. "I'm Shelby, and I love *Flair* more than just about anything in the whole world!" She continued to pump Camellia's hand, smiling a wide toothy grin. Her green excited eyes were blinding.

"It's a pleasure to meet you Shelby," Camellia said, patting the girl's hand while removing her other one from the firm grasp.

"Oh, I'm sorry, I'm just so excited." Shelby reached under the counter and pulled out a cup, placing it in front of Camellia. "My mama owns this diner and she would whip my hide if she saw me behaving this way. Can I get you coffee?"

"That would be lovely."

Shelby grabbed a fresh pot and poured, her hand noticeably shaky. The broken pot and its scattered contents were still on the floor. "What in the world are you doing in Markleeville?"

"Living here, apparently," Camellia responded, taking the stool positioned in front of the cup and sipping her coffee. She noticed the handful of customers listening to their exchange, Shelby's loud enthusiasm garnering full attention. "My husband and I moved to town about a month ago."

"Well this is just the best day ever!" A thought crossed Shelby's mind then, because her smile disappeared as her brows knitted. "But *why* are you here?"

Camellia crossed her legs and slipped out of her jacket, placing it on her lap. "My husband got a job nearby with a radiology practice," she explained simply.

"Oh." Shelby leaned on her elbows, her eyes darting about Camellia's luxurious clothing. "I guess with all the technology available, you can edit a magazine from anywhere, huh?"

Camellia pressed her lips together. "Shelby, *Flair* doesn't exist anymore. The publishing company decided to eliminate it from their group of magazines."

Shelby's fist hit the counter, startling Camellia. "Are you shitting me?" She clapped a hand over her mouth as Camellia burst into laughter.

"Between you and me, Shelby, that was exactly my thought."

Camellia spent the rest of the afternoon drinking coffee and nibbling on a colorful fruit salad while she and Shelby talked all things fashion, beauty, and celebrity. She found out that Shelby's favorite label was Rodarte – very fashion forward, especially coming from a small town girl – she loved Gucci's ad campaigns, and she thought Jennifer Aniston was the quintessential It Girl. Camellia agreed with her on all parts, causing Shelby to once again shriek with pleasure. It was the most enjoyable day Camellia had experienced in months.

They parted ways with Camellia promising to return to the diner for lunch in two days. She would have liked to have seen Shelby the very next day, however, not only did Camellia not wish to appear too eager, she also needed time to muse about how this girl figured into her comeback plans.

It was impossible to deny Shelby's beauty. She went beyond attractive. From her wide-set green eyes and straight nose to her high cheekbones and symmetrical face, Shelby would look just as good in photos as her long, slender body would look on a runway. And her bubbly personality was the tape holding fast the perfect package. Shelby was muse worthy. And she had absolutely no idea.

That evening, Camellia filled in Henry on her discovery. "This girl really has it," she explained, her eyes bright. "She's stunning, but not in that just-another-beautiful-girl way. You cannot take your eyes off of her and you can't put your finger on why. That's what makes for an extraordinary face and an über-successful model."

Henry kissed Camellia on the forehead before adding wood to the cast-iron stove. The bright flames danced merrily. "It's just nice to see you smiling again," he said. "I support anything that makes you this happy."

Camellia spent the next day on the Internet, trying to determine the best route to take with Shelby. Perusing photos from the past year's catwalks and magazine editorials, a number of the images from back issues of *Flair*, Camellia studied the faces and bodies of the most in-demand models of the moment: Karlie Kloss, Chanel Iman,

Anja Rubik, Miranda Kerr. They all possessed the same winning combination of unforgettable looks and an inner glow that made them dazzle. Just like Shelby.

The way Camellia saw it, she could go two routes with the eighteen-year-old beauty: acting as her manager or starting a modeling agency built around a single superstar. Every agency had to start with one girl and then grow from there. Why couldn't she do it? Granted, this wasn't New York or LA or Miami or Chicago. Hell, where she was located in Michigan – just above the third knuckle of the mitten as Henry described it – felt like a world away from Detroit, which her research showed had several agencies in the city's suburbs, with a couple of their girls landing a few major fashion show bookings. With amazing photos of Shelby and her contacts there was a real chance Camellia could find Shelby plenty of work, and wind up with a nice commission and newfound respect from the fashion world. Camellia Rhodes could be the next great 'fashion eye" – finding the undiscovered gems and turning them into superstars. It would be quite rewarding, giving these young unknowns opportunities they could never fully imagine. And Camellia would once again have a full, exciting schedule.

Now that Henry was receiving a regular paycheck, and a nice one at that, Camellia could afford to have a logo and business cards created, along with a state-of-the-art website for her business, which she decided would be called The Rhodes Agency, keeping the business open for all types of talent, from models to actors.

She located a design firm in New York that she had worked with several times and spoke with one of the partners, arranging for them to start working immediately on her logo, which she expressed should be clean and modern in appearance. With a promise for a one-week turnaround of preliminary designs, Camellia ended the call feeling unbelievably satisfied. The next step was to approach Shelby.

At noon the following day, Camellia was back in the diner, as promised. Shelby was behind the counter, taking direction from a petite woman with graying hair at her temples and the same green eyes as Shelby. Camellia guessed this was Shelby's mother, the diner's owner, and apparently not where Shelby got her soaring height. Camellia took a table at the back, motioning to Shelby to join her. Within minutes, Shelby was at her side, looking rocker chic in black leggings, black embellished flat boots, and a little white tank, with silver chains dangling past her bust, which Camellia guessed was about a 34A, perfect for runway, but not right for Victoria's Secret. "Sit," Camellia said, patting the seat beside her. "I have an amazing opportunity for you."

Shelby's face flushed. "For me? Oh my gosh, what is it?" She slid into the seat and crossed her legs gracefully.

"Shelby, have you ever considered modeling?"

The flush on Shelby's cheeks turned crimson, and she put a hand over her mouth, hiding her adorable gap-toothed smile. "Are you kidding?" she replied, her voice muffled behind the still-in-place hand.

Camellia pulled Shelby's hand down and placed it between her own. "I'm not kidding. I've been in this business a long time, and I know a model when I see one."

Shelby's giggles were contagious; Camellia couldn't help but laugh along with her. "Come on," Shelby managed, genuinely surprised. "Me?"

"Yes you. What do you think about giving it a try? I'm starting my own agency and you can be the first girl I sign. Before you know it, you'll be walking alongside Gisele and Naomi."

That did it. Shelby's shriek turned every head in the diner. She seemed to have a knack for it. "Miss Rhodes, I'm going to cry!" And then she did.

"Thanks for the heads up," Camellia chuckled, patting Shelby on the arm. She noticed the woman behind the counter, who was rather skinny upon closer look, was watching them intently. "Is that your mom?" Camellia asked, nodding in the woman's direction.

Shelby turned and gave the woman, who was now positively frowning, a little wave. "Yep, that's my mama. Sharene Rosalee Jenkins. Wanna meet her?"

"Maybe another time. When's your next day off?" Camellia thought it best to wrap up the conversation. She didn't want to be the reason Shelby was neglecting the other customers. A good agent knew better than to get on the bad side of a model's mom.

"Thursday," Shelby sputtered.

The day before Valentine's Day, Camellia thought. "Be at my house at ten," she said, writing her address down on a slip of paper she pulled from her handbag. "We'll begin model training then."

Camellia left the diner, careful to nod pleasantly at Shelby's mother, and turned right, heading four doors down to Lisa's Designs, one of the two women's boutiques in town. The opportunity she had found in Shelby had cheered Camellia enough to attempt shopping in an unknown store with a window of outdated clothing.

"Welcome to Lisa's Designs. I'm Lisa! How can I help you today?"

Camellia eyed the owner, who was sporting a close-cropped cut and wire-rimmed glasses. Her clothing paralleled the items in the window: beige pleated pants, an off-white blouse, and an embroidered vest depicting playful cats. "I'm...just looking." Camellia was regretting entering the shop but didn't want to be rude and bolt.

"That's just fine," Lisa said, not appearing to pick up on Camellia's hesitation. "Have a look around, and don't miss our Panty Bonanza next to the register. All the undies you can fit into a Ziploc for only $9.99."

"Uh, thanks," Camellia said, stifling a laugh. "I'll keep that in mind." She wandered around, trying not to touch the racks of acrylic sweaters and polyester-blend pants. In the back corner of the store, she found was she was looking for. Sort of. The available lingerie wasn't quite what she had in mind to surprise Henry for Valentine's Day. The bras were heavy duty, with wide straps and four rows of hooks. Nightgowns were full length and made of flannel. Apparently all the underwear were participating in the Panty Bonanza, as there was no selection with the rest of the unmentionables. However there were numerous half-slips, all plain and either in white or cream.

Feeling particularly mischievous, Camellia pulled a few items from the rack, and then stopped at the Panty Bonanza – which was complete with a blue flashing police light – cramming four pairs of briefs into a sandwich bag before placing her finds on the counter.

"Ooh, this looks like a successful shopping trip!" Lisa exclaimed.

"It certainly was," Camellia said, rolling her eyes as Lisa bent down for a shopping bag.

Lisa rang up Camellia's items and packed them in a bright pink bag. She walked the bag around the counter and handed it to Camellia, just like a salesperson at a high-end boutique would, which caught Camellia's attention. "Have you ever worked for Neiman Marcus or Bergdorf Goodman?" she asked.

"Nordstrom actually, just outside Detroit," Lisa answered, her face puzzled.

"I could tell you were trained properly," Camellia said, holding up the bag as explanation. "How did you get here?"

"My husband took the early retirement option from GM, and with the kids grown and living all over the country, we decided to sell the house and move to Paradise."

"And your car broke down in Markleeville so you stayed?" Camellia blushed at her remark. "I'm sorry. We relocated here in January and I'm having some trouble acclimating."

"Ah, no worries, honey. Markleeville certainly isn't everyone's cup of tea. You've got to love small-town living, because this is one small town. Where did you move from?"

"New York."

"Oh, well, then you certainly are experiencing some culture shock, aren't you?"

Camellia nodded, fighting back tears. "I didn't pay attention to exactly *where* in Michigan we were going. I had some...things happening at the time." She sniffed, her lower lip starting to quiver. Lisa pulled a tissue from behind the counter and handed it to her. "Thanks," Camellia said, her attempt at a smile looking more like a pout. "I went online and found amazing shopping and dining in Michigan: Gucci and Louis Vuitton and beautiful wine bars. What I didn't find was *this*."

"Oh yes, I know the area that you're speaking of. Unfortunately, it's a good three hours from Markleeville." Lisa's smile was warm and filled with understanding. "What's your name, honey?"

"Camellia."

"Camellia, you know the first step in getting to like a new place?" Camellia shook her head in response. "Finding a new friend. How about you come by my house for lunch next week?"

Lisa's attention was briefly torn away from Camellia to wave enthusiastically at a bundled-up woman scurrying past, her nose and a slice of cheek peeking out from a bulky hood trimmed in fake fur. "That was Tina, my scrapbooking partner," she explained.

The thought of an afternoon filled with crafting conversation and peanut butter sandwiches snapped Camellia from her vulnerable state. "It's getting late," she said, backing away from Lisa. "It was lovely to meet you. I'm consumed with a large project at the moment, but perhaps after."

"Sure," Lisa replied, her dark eyes knowing. "Perhaps after."

FIFTEEN

Shelby was prompt, an excellent quality for a model in training. Camellia greeted her wearing wide-legged trousers and a creamy cashmere sweater, her growing hair pulled into a messy chignon. She was embarrassed, to say the least, to have Shelby see where she lived, but she and Henry had agreed to wait until spring before they started looking for their own home – both understandably concerned about what might be hidden under several inches of snow.

"Your house is adorable!" Shelby exclaimed, looking around. "No way! We have the same couch!"

"Imagine that," Camellia said, taking Shelby's puffy parka and hanging it on the coat rack. "It's a rental. None of the furniture is ours, actually."

"Bummer," Shelby said. She looked unsure of herself, standing in the middle of the living room, her hands intertwined as she shifted her weight from one foot to the other. "So, what do we do first?" she asked, cocking her head to the side.

"Let's start with posture." Camellia stood in front of the girl.

"Stand up straight." The young girl did as Camellia commanded, earning her a frown. "A model needs to stand with confidence," she explained, pushing Shelby's shoulders back and down, and lifting her chin. "You want to look strong, fierce, and in charge."

Shelby nodded yet looked wary. "It doesn't feel very natural."

"With practice, it will become second nature." Camellia floated gracefully into the kitchen and turned to face Shelby. "Now walk to me."

Shelby took a deep breath and shuffled over, stopping just before stepping on Camellia's toes. "How was that?"

"All wrong. Go back and watch me." Shelby groaned. "Just watch," Camellia said with authority, sending Shelby scurrying into the living room. Camellia stood tall; her head up and shoulders back. She took a light breath then burst forward, one leg quietly stomping in front of the other, her line perfectly straight. Upon reaching Shelby, she stopped, planting her left foot widely and leaning slightly from the waist in the direction of her planted foot, just long enough before pivoting on her right foot and marching back to the kitchen, her arms just barely swinging at her sides.

Shelby burst into applause. "Amazing!" she cried.

"Now you," Camellia said, switching in a nanosecond from model back to model agent.

Shelby puffed out her bottom lip. "Camellia, I don't know if I can do this."

"Nonsense. You're already two-thirds of the way to being a model. You have the look. You have the grace. Hell, you even dress like an off-duty model. Where do you shop, anyway?"

The pout was replaced with a wide grin. "Walmart!" she announced, sashaying about in her zipper-covered shirt, dark gray denim, and cropped motorcycle boots.

Camellia closed her eyes and pressed her fingers to the bridge of her nose, trying to ward off the sudden throbbing she felt in her head. "Anywhere else?" she asked hopefully.

"Nah, they pretty much have everything there." Shelby dumped her long body onto the couch, sinking in. "Where do you shop?"

"Lately? Nowhere."

"I'll bet your closet is so amazing, you don't need anything. Not a thing."

Camellia perched on the arm of the big blue chair. "Needing and wanting are two different things entirely."

Shelby leaned forward, her face bright. "Will you show me?"

"Show you?"

"Your closest. I won't take anything. I swear."

Camellia laughed softly. "Of course. But I warn you, it doesn't show very well. Closet space in this place is very limited. Two-thirds of my things are in storage and the rest is jammed into one rather unsatisfactory reach-in closet. It's a struggle to find anything." She led Shelby up the stairway, into the bedroom, throwing open creaky bi-fold doors. "Have at it," she said.

Shelby gasped. "Oh Camellia, I could cry!" she gushed, taking in the closet's contents, from the line of handbags on the top shelf to the three neat rows of shoes consuming every inch of the floor.

Camellia winced at the state of her wrinkled clothing hanging on top of one another. "Yep. Me too."

"May I?" Shelby asked, her eyes filled with anticipation.

Camellia nodded, and Shelby began pulling out dresses, blouses, skirts, and trousers. Every item she took into her hands was met with a mix of whimpering and delight. "So beautiful!" she cried, pulling out a structured Prada dress and carefully hugging it, only to be distracted by turquoise snakeskin sandals at her feet. "No way — Fendi platforms!" Shelby bent down to get a better look, caressing the shoes as if stroking the fur of a cat. "Oh! Is that Valentino?" she asked, forgetting the shoes and reaching up for a red leather tote with an enormous matching leather flower that was tucked into a corner of the closet. She slid the handles onto her shoulder and stood to better admire the bag in a propped up full-length mirror set to the left of the closet. "It's just the most gorgeous thing I've ever seen!" she exclaimed, turning in a circle to catch the bag at every angle.

It was fun for Camellia to observe Shelby's fresh look at pieces she'd worn or carried dozens of times without putting much thought into them. Being constantly cloaked in designer goods had long been second nature. The clothing allowance she had while at *Flair*, along with regular gifts she received from top designers around the globe, allowed her to dress in the newest and most sought-after designs. She had forgotten what it was like to desire beautiful clothes that were beyond her budget. "Do you love it?" Camellia asked, nodding at the handbag.

"More than my own breath," Shelby declared dramatically.

"Then it's yours."

Shelby froze. "What?"

"Valentino should only be owned by a woman who truly understands its magnificence."

"Oh Camellia, I couldn't."

"You can. And you will. It's a gift to mark your first day of your journey to becoming a model." Camellia kicked the Fendi platforms back into the closet and closed the doors. "One day, when you're getting booked for fashion weeks all over the world, you'll have your own closetful of couture. Consider this bag a symbol of what that life has to offer you."

Shelby scrunched her shoulders to her ears and smiled wide. "It sounds like a dream."

"It *is* a dream. Now, back downstairs," Camellia ordered, motioning with a graceful hand. "Your runway awaits."

Henry cooked for Valentine's Day, an impressive spread of roast turkey, brown sugar baked sweet potatoes, and a salad with toasted celery seeds. Camellia set the table, admiring the full white roses Henry had picked up after work. "I haven't come across a flower shop around here, so I'm guessing the hospital has its own," Camellia noted, folding cloth napkins.

"Actually, they were closed by the time I left. Luckily Walmart has a big selection."

Camellia groaned, dropping into a chair at the end of the table. "Henry, does *all* of our shopping have to take place at Walmart?"

Henry set two shallow bowls filled with salad on top of their plates, then produced a folded piece of paper from his shirt pocket. "Not *all* our shopping," he said, handing the paper to Camellia.

Puzzled, she unfolded the paper and studied its contents. Then she gasped. "You bought us lakefront property?" she asked, hopeful.

"It's not a done deal yet," he explained, taking the seat next to her. "After botching this place, I wasn't going to sign anything without first getting your consent. Can I take you to see it this weekend?"

"Yes!" Camellia cried, throwing her arms around her husband. "Tell me more."

"It's a nice parcel of land on Parson's Lake. Very picturesque."

"I've heard that one before," Camellia said, fetching a bottle of Cabernet from the counter.

"For real this time," Henry assured. "There's a tired old house there now, but we can have that torn down and then build whatever we want. In fact, about half the houses at the lake are new builds."

"So we can make it whatever we want?"

"Pretty much. That's why I wasn't worried about waiting until spring. We're going to bulldoze the current structure anyway. Once we have a deal we can meet with an architect and create the house of our dreams."

Camellia held her wine glass up. "We need a toast." Henry raised his glass as well, gazing lovingly at his wife. "To the best Valentine's Day present ever."

"Is it better than roses from Walmart?" Henry teased.

"Slightly. Now I wish I'd done more with your present."

Henry's eyes widened. "Dare I ask?"

"You'll see for yourself after dinner."

With a bottle of port and two glasses in hand, Henry led Camellia upstairs. "Enough anticipation," Henry said breathily in his wife's ear. "I'm more than ready for my present."

"You better fill up your glass then," she replied mysteriously, picking up the bright pink bag from the bed and slipping into the bathroom. She emerged a few minutes later wearing a red and blue plaid flannel nightgown with a ruffled collar and sleeves.

In mid-sip, Henry nearly spit out the port on the patchwork quilt. "What in the hell is that?" he croaked.

"This," Camellia cooed, flirtatiously lifting the heavy gown to reveal her ankles then sashaying over to the bed, "is the hottest lingerie trend in Markleeville."

"Oh, is it now?" Henry chuckled, grabbing for the heavy fabric.

Camellia slapped away Henry's hand. "Please! I believe you are misinterpreting the trend."

"And what is this trend, exactly?" He reached for her again, but this time was shut down by Camellia pulling the nightgown firmly over her knees and tucking the bottom under her feet.

"Why, schoolmarm chic, don't you know?" She laughed, her eyes wide. "Oddly, I think you're rather aroused."

Henry tugged at the nightgown, freeing Camellia's legs. He grabbed them and pulled her closer to him. "Maybe these Markleeville folks are onto something. And," he said, reaching behind her to unbutton the back of the nightgown, "your newest claim to fame can be introducing the schoolmarm chic look to the masses. Designers everywhere will be kicking themselves that they didn't come up with it first."

Camellia giggled. "Yes, I can see Chanel doing it in a black and white tweed. It will be all the rage."

Reaching his hands past her thighs, Henry suddenly stopped and lifted the nightgown, his expression perplexed. "Honey, your underwear are enormous," he said matter-of-fact.

Camellia broke into a fit of laughter, rolling right off the bed.

SIXTEEN

That weekend, Henry drove Camellia to Parson's Lake, a ten-minute drive east of town. While the scenery along the way was just as woodsy and rural as the rest of Markleeville, upon reaching the lake, the real estate changed dramatically. The dwellings nearest to town were still small and shack-like, however, the houses bordering the far side of the lake were new and grand, with private docks and impressive multi-level decks. Camellia's heart swelled.

Henry stopped the car about halfway along the west side of the lake, pulling into the driveway of a dilapidated wooden structure on a large, flat parcel of land.

"I can't believe I'm saying this, but I'd much rather live in our cottage in downtown Markleeville than that rundown shanty, even on such a beautiful lake," Camellia noted, frowning at the asphalt roof that was starting to cave in.

"Thankfully, you won't have to do either. In less than nine months, we can have this shack knocked down and a gorgeous four bedroom, three bath home standing in its place."

"I can barely believe it."

"Come on." Henry shut off the car, and the pair trudged through the snow around the back of the structure. The view was breathtaking, even on such an overcast day: the expansive water partially frozen and Zen-like, a gaggle of geese in flight overhead. The backdrop of fine homes was proof that civilized life was possible high up in Michigan's mitten.

"I don't get it," Camellia said. "All these amazing homes. How come I never run into these people in town?"

"Because a number of them are summer homes," Henry reminded. "Just wait. Once the weather warms up, it's going to be a different world here."

"Hmm." Camellia wasn't as worried as she once was to find people more like her in Markleeville. She had Shelby now. She had purpose. That was all she needed at the moment. That and the promise of a new home with Henry.

The following week, Shelby was ready for the next steps in her walk: adding music and getting some elevation. That Saturday night, after closing time at the diner, Camellia and Shelby stood on top of the counter, Rihanna's "Don't Stop the Music" blaring from the old radio. Only the counter lights were turned on, illuminating the makeshift runway. Dressed in her uniform of skinny denim and slouchy t-shirt, Shelby was also sporting four-inch Louboutin pumps on loan from Camellia.

"Models fall off runways," Camellia spoke over Rihanna's sexy whine. "Your job is to get so comfortable at this height, that a couple feet off the ground is child's play to you."

Shelby nodded but looked unsure. "What if I fall?"

"You won't. Watch your feet the first couple of times. Count your steps. Know where you are the entire time and you won't fall."

"Okay." Shelby moved slowly, as uncomfortable with the counter height as she was with her heel height. "Guess I need to give my flat boots a rest," she called out, teetering along at a slow pace.

Camellia watched her student's unsteady progress. "It's all about getting comfortable in a new situation. You may feel out of your element at first, but eventually, if you keep working at it, you find your stride."

Shelby kept at it for the next hour, each time down the counter becoming more natural and less scary. And then, in the middle of Estelle's "American Boy", Shelby did find her stride. With chin raised and shoulders back, she marched along the counter, with just the right amount of sway in her hips, hitting the end with a confident pose before pivoting and strutting back to Camellia, who flung her arms around Shelby in approval. A knock on the diner window pulled them from their celebration, and they turned to find a tall boy with messy chestnut-brown hair waving timidly at them.

"Friend of yours?" Camellia asked, noticing the blush on Shelby's cheeks.

"Justin," she whispered, unable to take her eyes off the boy.

Camellia stepped back and crossed her arms. "I think we're done here. Why don't you take off?"

Shelby bit her bottom lip. "Are you sure?" Her voice was hopeful.

"Yep," Camellia replied, helping Shelby out of her shoes so she could climb down from the counter. "I'll see you next week for photo posing. Oh wait." She reached into the pocket of her blazer and pulled out a thin stack of cards. "My new business cards," she said, handing them to Shelby. "Just on the off chance you run into anyone even half as stunning as you."

Shelby smiled and shoved the cards deep into the pocket of her jeans. She pulled on her boots and grabbed her jacket and shoulder bag, digging around to locate the diner keys. She shut off the counter light and opened the door for Camellia, locking it behind them. Before Camellia could say another word, Shelby had already reached the boy, his hands lightly grazing her elbows, their smiles broad. *They're sweet*, Camellia thought, remembering the look of young love. She hoped the boy would understand when Shelby relocated to New York. Infatuation was adorable at eighteen, but it couldn't hold a candle to the life of an in-demand model.

SEVENTEEN

"Can I steal you away from your star pupil for an evening? We've been invited to a dinner party." Henry said, rolling on top of Camellia and pinning her arms above her head.

"Dinner party?" Camellia said, intrigued. "I'm listening."

Henry kissed her along her neck, pausing at her ear, his hot breath making her squirm. "At the home of our radiology group's director." He added, "On the lake."

"With real refined people?" Camellia teased, kissing Henry full on the mouth.

"But, of course, my love. Refinement is the main course, with a slice of civility for dessert." He let go of her arms and then led one south to his unzipped trousers. "It's tomorrow night at seven," he said, his voice husky.

Camellia pushed Henry off of her and sat up in bed. "Tomorrow night? Henry, have you seen my hair?" Her once glossy bob was now hanging lifeless below her shoulders, her dark roots taking up a significant portion of the top of her head.

"So go to the salon," Henry replied matter-of-fact. "There's one right in town. I'm sure they'll make you good as new." He pulled her on top of him. "Meanwhile, tonight, I'll be making you good as new in a different way."

"You are a cocky thing, aren't you?" she cooed, succumbing to her husband's touch. She supposed it was about time she patronized more of Markleeville's businesses. Not everything could be as bad as the diner's weak coffee.

At ten a.m. the following morning, Camellia stood in front of the town's only beauty salon, regrettably named Do or Dye. For a moment, she considered taking her business to the barber shop next door, which was literally called The Barber Shop Next Door, but then decided the only thing barbers would know to do with foil was wrap a sandwich, so into Do or Dye she went.

A twenty-something girl stationed at the desk looked up at Camellia, her hair's high-contrast mix of platinum blonde and black stopping Camellia in her tracks. "Do you have an appointment?" the girl asked, her tone bored.

Camellia glanced around the salon. A frail, elderly woman with tightly wound, blue-gray hair occupied one of six chairs, her hairdresser, clad in tapered jeans and a polo shirt, conversing with her loudly. Camellia was wondering if the old lady's hair was at the before or after stage, when the hairdresser stepped behind her client and removed the brown cape from around her neck. "Oh God," Camellia said, not intentionally meaning to make her dread public.

"Well hi there! Would you like a haircut today?" A raspy voice startled Camellia, and she turned to see a chubby woman of about thirty-five with thick, dark hair and a fringe of bangs. She held out her hand to Camellia. "I'm Deb, the owner."

Camellia took a step back. "Um, no, actually," she said, her voice wavering. "I think I'm in the wrong place. Sorry." She fled to the diner, nearly colliding with Shelby at the door.

"Where are you off to in such a rush?" Shelby said brightly.

"Thank God you're here," Camellia said, taking Shelby by the arm. "I need your help."

After a quick trip to the pharmacy, they were back at Camellia's house, gathered at the kitchen counter with a box of at-home hair coloring. "Why do you trust me over someone who went to school for this?" Shelby questioned, tearing open the box and unfolding a large direction sheet.

"You had to see them. You would have understood," Camellia said, shuddering as she recalled the experience.

Shelby slipped on the plastic gloves that were included in the box. "See who? Deb? She's been doing my hair since I was thirteen."

"Really?" Camellia promenaded around Shelby for a closer inspection of her hair. "Okay, but you don't get your hair colored, do you?"

"No, but I have thought about it. Wouldn't I look great with copper-colored hair?"

"No." Camellia put a dark towel around her shoulders and sat on a high chair beside the peninsula. "You were born with perfect coloring. Don't change a thing."

"Ah, thanks!" Shelby expertly poured the contents of a tube into a half-filled bottle, put a finger over the tiny opening, and shook until the contents were blended.

"How do you know what you're doing?"

Shelby carried the container over to Camellia and began carefully squeezing the contents onto her roots and rubbing it in gently with her index finger. "I've been coloring my mom's hair forever. Then last month, she decided not to do it anymore. I guess she's finally accepted the gray," she said, working quickly. "Now that I think about it, I might be better at this than Deb. But don't tell her I said that."

Camellia appreciated that Shelby treated her warmly, rather than with a distance and respect that a mentor of her caliber usually received. Most girls who had interacted with Camellia had been either starstruck, terribly intimidated, or both. While Shelby was certainly a fan of *Flair*, and very aware of Camellia's significance in the fashion world, her demeanor was always welcoming and downright friendly. Camellia was grateful for that, considering that Shelby was the closest interpretation she had of a friend.

Once Shelby had the coloring worked through Camellia's hair, she set the oven timer and discarded the used bottles in the trash. "Twenty minutes and you'll be a new woman," she said.

"I don't know about new, but hopefully improved," Camellia mused, stepping down from the chair to put on a pot of coffee. "Tell me about your mom," she said suddenly.

The question elicited a big smile from Shelby. "She's amazing,"

Shelby said, taking a seat on the other side of the peninsula. "It's been just the two of us since I was a baby, and she's always been there for me."

"Since you were a baby?"

"Yeah, my dad – Richie – died in a hunting accident just before my first birthday." Camellia looked horrified, causing Shelby to shake her head. "No, he wasn't shot with a rifle or anything gruesome like that. He fell from a tree."

"Hunting from a tree?"

"He was in a tree stand, waiting for deer. My mama said one of his buddies admitted he had been drinking all afternoon, so he probably lost his footing. Broke his neck in the fall."

"That's awful." Camellia set out cups, sugar, and milk, trying to imagine a childhood without a parent. While her parents never understood her, at least they were always there to take care of her.

"I guess so. But I wasn't aware, you know? And, with my mama, I never felt like I was missing something."

"Have you told her about modeling?"

"Of course," Shelby said, emphatically. "I tell her everything."

"And what does she think?"

Shelby thought for a second, her brow furrowed. "Well, she hasn't said much about it, actually. She's been so busy getting the diner ready to sell."

"She's selling the diner?" The coffeemaker beeped, signaling the end of the brew cycle, and Camellia fetched it, pouring the hot liquid into both of their cups.

Shelby nodded. "Yes. She and my daddy opened the diner right after they got married. She says she's been at it long enough."

Camellia sipped her coffee deep in thought. "It's funny how things work out, isn't it? Just when your mom is selling the diner, you end up with an exciting new endeavor to pursue."

"I guess you're right."

Before long, the oven timer was dinging, pulling them from their conversation. "Time to rinse!" Shelby exclaimed, taking a quick slurp from her cup before slipping the plastic gloves back on her hands.

After Camellia was rinsed, conditioned, and rinsed again, Shelby towel-dried her mentor's hair before the women marched upstairs to check out the results in the bathroom mirror.

"You look great as a brunette," Shelby noted, as Camellia examined Shelby's work. "But why did you switch from the red? It was your signature."

"I didn't think I could manage a realistic red from an at-home kit," Camellia explained, retrieving the hair dryer from under the sink. "Besides, this is more like my natural color. I had forgotten what I used to look like."

Shelby grinned and checked her phone. "If it's okay, I'd better get going. I have a date with Justin in about an hour."

"Of course. What are you two doing today?" Camellia followed Shelby back down the stairs, Shelby grabbing her down jacket and the Valentino bag from the coat rack.

"Taking a drive to Cadillac to see a movie. Maybe pizza, too. How about you?"

"I'll be searching my closet for something to wear to a dinner party at the lake tonight."

"Oh, hanging out with The Snobs, huh?"

Camellia chuckled. "The Snobs?"

"That's what we call the lake people," Shelby explained, zipping her jacket. "The ones who live there year-round, anyway. They don't like us town people. Always looking at us up and down like we've got the plague."

Camellia felt her cheeks flush, suddenly ashamed of reacting in that very way to both Lisa and Deb. "I'm sure they're not all snobs," she suggested, a mix of hope and defensiveness evident in her voice.

"Oh yes, all of them. You'll see for yourself tonight."

Camellia gave Shelby a hug and opened the door for her, waving as the young beauty bounded down the front steps. She decided the news of her future move to the lake could wait for another day.

EIGHTEEN

Camellia emerged from the car, teetering in her Jimmy Choo stiletto booties up the icy pathway of an imposing contemporary house belonging to David Farling, director of Diagnostic Radiology Services. Her heart was beating with the intensity of a hip-hop bass line. Finally, after two months in Markleeville, she was coming face-to-face with women of her standing. She tightened the leather belt on her black mink coat as Henry pressed the bell.

They were received by a bald man in his sixties, clad in a brown sweater, brown trousers, and brown socks. "Finally, we get to meet the wife," he said, reaching out a hand to Camellia. "Cecilia, right?"

"Camellia, actually." She shook his hand firmly. "It's a pleasure to meet you."

"David is not only the director of the practice, he's also responsible for hiring me," Henry explained, helping Camellia out of her coat.

"Well, we sure have a lot to thank you for, don't we?"

Only Henry appeared to pick up on Camellia's sugary sarcasm, and he gave her a quick pinch on her backside in response.

"I know how to pick 'em," David said, patting Henry on the back. "Let me call my wife over. She's been waiting to meet you."

"Oh," Camellia said, pleased. "Okay—"

"Geri!" David bellowed, turning toward the crowd to summon his wife.

"You did say these were refined people, right?" Camellia whispered in Henry's ear.

"I had to get you here some way," he joked.

Coming towards them was a thin woman with long features and a short bob with bangs in the manner of Anna Wintour, clad in a St. John pantsuit. Camellia could recognize a St. John woman anywhere: sophisticated and timeless, and often loyally dressed head-to-toe in the knitwear label.

Geri held out an equally long hand, not a hint of a smile to be found on her face. "How do you do," she said matter-of-fact. "Excuse my husband's lack of tact," she added, as if apologizing for David was her norm de rigueur.

"That's quite all right," Camellia offered, wondering if Geri was embarrassed or just cold by nature.

"Champagne is being passed, otherwise there's a bartender stationed at the far end of the living room. Now, if you'll excuse me, there's a popover crisis in the kitchen that I must attend to." Geri's whip of a figure pivoted and gracefully hurried away, leaving Camellia behind with her mouth hanging open.

"Well then," David said, slapping Henry on the back again, "How about that booze?" He shuffled away without waiting for a response.

Camellia stepped into the living room with Henry right behind her. The space was spectacular, with unfussy cream sofas and chairs set off by striped pillows and rich woods; the impressive floor-to-ceiling windows allowing a breathtaking view of the lake. Small groups of guests stood in tight circles, closing off their low-key conversations from each other.

In New York, Camellia used to walk into parties such as this, expecting every circle to immediately widen in welcome of her presence, which they did. Manicured hands would wave her over, hoping to be the first she acknowledged. The most difficult decisions of her evening had been where to start and how long to linger before moving on to the next cluster of guests.

Here, however, the mood was very different. No one seemed to notice she was in the room, even though she stood out from the affluent crowd. While the women were obviously clothed in expensive labels, their uninspired manner of dressing – predominately in black and rigorously matched – left Camellia's modern mixed prints looking as if she hadn't received the memo on proper lakefront party attire.

Henry snatched two glasses of champagne from a waiter passing by, handing one to Camellia. "Come on, let me make some introductions." He took her hand and led her to the closest group, nodding at a man in a black polo and matching trousers. "Stephan," Henry called out, letting go of Camellia's hand to shake his. "This is my wife Camellia."

"Good to meet you," Stephan said, stepping back just enough to let Henry and Camellia squeeze into the circle. Stephan's attention turned back to the conversation in progress, which Camellia quickly picked up was regarding a new Chief of Staff at Mercy Hospital, who was trying to change much of the protocol after a week on the job. She observed as all the men chatted easily, apparently all radiologists, as the women stood beside their husbands, politely nodding and sipping their champagne. *What is this, Stepford?* Camellia thought, wondering if the wives did anything other than keep house and press their husbands' clothing.

As the evening progressed, Henry moved Camellia from circle to circle, where she caught a couple of doctors' names, listened to medical conversations that were mostly over her head, and attempted with little luck not to appear bored. Two hours into the party, she slipped away from a conversation about pharmaceutical reps and wandered over to the bar for something stronger.

"Can I get a whiskey?" she said, hoping she didn't sound as desperate as she felt.

A woman in a simple black dress with a strand of pearls at her neck appeared next to her. "Gin and tonic," she said forcefully, apparently not concerned with waiting her turn.

Though Camellia didn't like the woman's gruff behavior, she was her only opportunity so far for a one-on-one conversation. She took the rocks glass from the bartender and turned to face the woman. "I'm Camellia," she said, holding out her hand. "My husband Henry started with the practice in early January."

The woman eyed her warily and offered a limp hand in return. "Cassandra Ward," she said coolly, turning back to watch the bartender make her drink. "I hear you're living in town. What's *that* like?"

"Small," Camellia admitted, sipping her whiskey.

"I imagine so," Cassandra said, gingerly taking the finished gin and tonic from the bartender and eyeing it just as warily. "Have a good evening," she said, not particularly addressing either Camellia or the bartender, and walked away.

After three grueling hours, Camellia flashed Henry her take-me-home-now look and walked to the foyer for her coat, leaving Henry to bid their hosts farewell. She couldn't take another strained minute. He practically carried her back to the car, knowing full well what Camellia looked like when she was about to combust, and obviously not wanting that to occur within earshot of his colleagues. He drove as quickly as the icy roads would allow, as an enraged Camellia dramatically recounted their first party at the lake.

"Am I missing something? I mean seriously, what don't I know about these women? Henry, they're so mean!" She switched off the heat, feeling feverish. "I kept wondering: Am I doing something insulting? Was I supposed to remove my shoes? Do I match the description of a serial child killer? What was it? What had I done to make these women shut me out upon introduction?"

"I don't know. I really don't know," Henry said. "While I don't know any of the wives, I can tell you that the guys in my group are all pretty decent human beings."

"And what's with all the doctors being men and all the women being, well, the *little women*? It's like I stepped back in time in there."

"Kind of Stepford-like, wasn't it?" Henry conceded.

"That's what I thought!" Camellia reached up and began pulling out hairpins, releasing her hair from the messy bun she had created for the evening. "Honestly Henry, if I wanted to be treated this way, I would have gladly stayed in New York."

"Maybe they're intimidated by you."

"Intimidated by an out-of-work editor with a contact list full of high-profile celebrities who wouldn't call her back if her hair was on fire?"

"No, intimidated by what you built; what you've accomplished. And, of course, how freaking gorgeous you are."

Camellia had to smile. Henry always had her back. "They obviously know something about me. That one evil thing, Cassandra Ward, was fully aware we were living in town. Which apparently, in their set, is frowned upon."

"I can understand that," Henry said, turning into their driveway, which suddenly felt like a haven to Camellia. "After all, we do have easy access to the best big-girl panties around."

NINETEEN

Shelby's mood wasn't right when she arrived at Camellia's house the following week to practice posing for photos. Instead of her customary jovial greeting, she barely managed a terse smile as she pushed passed Camellia and dropped into the oversized living room chair.

Camellia bit her lip, studying her pupil for a minute, and then perched on the arm of the sofa. "What's on your mind?" she asked in a gentle voice.

"I'm not really sure," Shelby said weakly.

"Boy trouble?"

Shelby shook her head. "No, things are fine with Justin." She looked up at Camellia, her eyes holding all her sorrow. "It's my mom."

"Your mom?"

"Yeah. She was clearly not happy that I was coming to your house today."

Camellia cocked her head to the side. "Did she say why?"

"No. That's the thing." Shelby shifted in the chair, tucking a long leg under her. "We had breakfast and folded laundry and we talked like we normally do. Then I told her all about New York, and she got really quiet. And really cold." Her eyes welled with tears. "Camellia, she's never been like that with me before. Never."

"I'm sorry." Camellia leaned back and grabbed a compact camera from the coffee table. "Maybe she's just worried," she suggested, turning on the camera and quickly capturing Shelby's misery.

"Delete that," Shelby said, wiping a rogue tear. She sniffed then wiped at her nose, too. "Why would she be worried? You're a prominent editor, not some skanky old man trying to photograph me naked."

"Was," Camellia noted, sliding onto the floor to snap more photos from a lower angle. "Moms worry, Shelby, and you're her only child *to* worry about. You have an exciting life ahead of you in New York. That can be a very tough scenario for a mom to take, especially if she's feeling left behind."

Shelby popped up and slapped her thighs. "That's it. She thinks I'm abandoning her. That I'm going to run off to New York and forget all about her." She shook her head and smiled as if enjoying a private joke. "She's so silly."

Camellia continued taking pictures of Shelby's seemingly endless expressions, which was now transforming from a smug smile into something resembling a trance.

"Are you lost in thought?" Camellia asked from behind the camera.

Shelby snapped out of it and giggled, curling her lithe body around the arm of the chair. "There's no reason she couldn't move to New York with me, is there?"

Camellia lowered the camera, considering the question. "No, there really isn't, as long as she's willing. She *is* selling the diner, so there wouldn't be much tying her down here."

"Exactly!" Shelby bounded to her feet in one graceful move. "Do you mind if I go tell her the good news?"

"Do you mind getting through your primer on posing first?" Camellia asked authoritatively. "You're not going to be sought after as a model if you don't know what you're doing. Or if you can't focus."

Shelby obeyed, gingerly settling back into the chair. "Got it, Boss Lady. Where do we begin?"

Camellia turned the camera around for Shelby to see, scrolling through the photos she just took. "You photograph beautifully. There's no question. What's really important in these pictures is your expression. Do you see how believable you are?"

Pulling the camera closer, Shelby studied the photos. She nodded. "Sure. When I'm happy, I look happy. When I'm sad, I look sad."

"That's right." Camellia set the camera on the floor beside her. "It's easy to show what you're feeling. But what if a photographer wants you to appear happily in love, when in reality your boyfriend has just broken your heart?"

"That would be tough."

"Or, you just landed a fabulous apartment, are booked for work all month, and you can't stop smiling about it, and then you're asked to appear sullen and on the edge of tears. How do you find that expression and then convince the person viewing the picture that it's real?"

Shelby shrugged her shoulders. "Acting classes?"

"No. It's quite simple, actually. You find a memory that matches the expression you need to give, and you live in that memory as you're posing."

"What if I don't have a memory that matches?" Shelby questioned. "What if I've never been in love and have no idea what my face would look like if I were in love?"

"Then you imagine it. Whether it's from a love scene in a movie that affected you or it's from what you imagine it would feel like to be completely consumed by love, you go to that place and sink into it, and it will show on your face." Camellia rolled onto her knees, grabbed the camera, and held it to her face. "Okay, now let's see how well you listen to me."

Camellia spent the next month coaching Shelby, from how to follow a photographer's direction and what to expect at a go-see to putting together a portfolio and the ins and outs of living and working in New York. Once she was certain Shelby was ready for the next step, Camellia went in search of a photographer to create Shelby's comp card.

What she really wanted was to fly out Sylvia Steiner to photograph Shelby. Sylvia was a pro and had worked with nearly every supermodel in the business. She had also been responsible for photographing more than a dozen *Flair* covers. They had always worked so well together, and Camellia knew Sylvia would most certainly be up for the trip, especially it meant not only getting paid well but also having a hand in introducing the hottest new model to New York's fashion sect.

But Camellia couldn't do it. She couldn't risk bringing Sylvia to Markleeville – to have her witness the way she had been living for the last three months. If the lake house had been built, that would have been different. She pictured a stunning Hamptons-esque home with a glorious sailboat docked in back and a groomed-and-ready supermodel in the making, gracefully reclining in a vintage Eames chair positioned next to a roaring fire with a view of the lake. Now that was a scene in which Camellia would have happily welcomed any guest. But country furniture in a cramped cottage with a ghastly wood-burning stove? Sylvia, who conveniently always had a camera in hand, would have sent those images in a New York minute to every editor she knew. Sylvia Steiner may have once been something of a friend, but few could pass up sharing such a juicy discovery about Camellia Rhodes.

Instead, Camellia turned to a reputable online site that served as a source for models, photographers, and stylists to showcase their work, searchable by geographic location. In less than fifteen minutes she had found a photographer in Traverse City with a decent ability for capturing people.

She was in the middle of typing up an introductory email when Henry bounded through the door, holding daffodils wrapped in paper. Camellia was delighted. "Daffodil season," she said, accepting the flowers from her husband. "Spring must be around the corner."

He kissed her on the head. "Let's hope so, my dear. I am sick of snow." Removing his wet boots, Henry hung his jacket on the coat rack and then tended to the fire, which was only glowing embers. "Honey, you've got to keep this fire going during the day."

"I hate that thing."

"Yes, but if you put a log on from time to time, you wouldn't have to wear two sweaters and a scarf in the house."

"Luckily layering is in," she said, as her fingers resumed clicking along the keyboard. "Besides, we'll have a new house soon with a fireplace that operates via remote control. Now *that* I'll learn to use."

Henry closed the door of the wood stove and sat beside Camellia on the sofa. "That reminds me, the architect wants to come by this week to go over the plans."

Camellia's stopped typing. "They're done?"

"Yep. And the old shack has been demolished, too. I've been told we are going to be very pleased with the plans. It's a Cape Cod with edge. What do you think of that description?"

"I think it sounds truly fabulous." Camellia set her laptop on the coffee table, too excited about the house to concentrate on the letter. "Oh Henry," she said, throwing her legs over her husband's lap, "this feels like the start of us becoming us again."

"We've always been us, Camellia," he said, holding onto her legs. "Through our highest and lowest points, we're the one thing that has remained constant. A new house will be nice, but it's nothing compared to what we have in each other."

"Henry." Camellia was beyond touched. She was also aware just how right he was. They had been through extraordinarily shitty times. And their marriage had never faltered. Even during the past six years at *Flair* as she transformed from merely confident and opinionated into a cold know-it-all. She was crazy lucky to have found him at that fateful photo shoot for *Elle*. *The rising-star photographer and the outspoken junior fashion editor*, she thought, grinning. It had the makings of a teen romance novel. Maybe once Shelby was well on her way to supermodel status, Camellia would try her hand at penning the story.

And then an even better idea popped into Camellia's head. She whipped her legs off of Henry and knelt on the couch, taking her husband's face in her hands. "Remember when you said you'd support anything that made me as happy as working with Shelby?"

"Yes," Henry said cautiously, "I remember."

"Then dust off your camera, Henry Rhodes. There's a model-to-be in need of an eye like yours."

TWENTY

The photos were everything Camellia had hoped for. Creating a makeshift studio in the garage, using old bed sheets and found construction materials for backdrops, along with a few shots in the woods behind the house and in neighboring fields, Henry had created magical portraits that emphasized Shelby's unique beauty and transformative ability. Camellia had played a major role as well, applying Shelby's makeup and working her hair into updos, playful braids, and long, lovely waves. She styled the girl in her own dresses, trousers, and blouses, utilizing Shelby's bikini and youthful rompers for more skin-baring looks.

Shelby had been a real pro, never letting the camera see how cold she really was, as the frigid wind whipped her hair and tore at her exposed skin.

After nearly a full day of posing, Henry wrapped the shoot, and escorted the chilled women back into the house where he stoked the fire, ordered veggie pizzas, and downloaded the images to Camellia's laptop.

The three poured over the photos as they ate, Henry narrowing down the pictures little by little until they were left with the final selections.

"You're still amazing at this Henry," Camellia noted, pulling a red pepper from her slice and chewing it delicately.

Shelby nodded in agreement. "I can't believe you used to shoot covers for all the big fashion magazines," she swooned.

"That feels like a lifetime ago," Henry said, folding his pizza in half and taking a big bite.

"Do you ever regret leaving all the glamour for hospitals and sick people?" Shelby questioned.

Henry chuckled. "Honestly? No. While I recognized I was good at it, my heart wasn't in it."

"Well, I think you're a nut job, but to each their own. At least that's what my mama's always telling me."

"Speaking of your mother, are things better?" Camellia asked, dabbing the sides of her mouth with a paper napkin.

Shelby beamed. "Oh yes. I told her she could move to New York with me and she hugged me and cried and cried and cried."

"That's good news," Camellia said, rising from her seat to clear the plates. "If she's happy to hear that, just wait until she sees your photos."

"She's going to lose her mind!" Shelby jumped up to help. "So what's next?"

"Next I'll send the photo choices, along with your name, measurements, and my contact information to the printer, and in a couple of weeks you'll have comp cards. We'll also get an electronic version that we can email to designers and fashion and beauty editors. My website is ready, so I can promote you there, too."

"Awesome!" Shelby grabbed a roll of tinfoil from the counter and wrapped the leftover pizza, storing it in the refrigerator. "Is it okay if I split?" she asked. "I told Justin I'd try to meet up with him tonight."

"Sure," Camellia said. "I'll email you images to show your mom. Other than that, you get a little modeling break until your comp cards are in. It won't last long, so enjoy it while you can."

Thankfully, Camellia had the new house to keep her busy while waiting for the comp cards to arrive. She and Henry had a productive meeting with the architect, a competent, no-nonsense woman in her thirties, who drove in from Traverse City to present her plans.

The house was perfect: a four thousand-square-foot home with a two-story ceiling in the spacious living room and two sets of French doors leading to a screened-in porch that ran the length of the house. The gourmet kitchen featured a sizable island, a small sitting area with a stone fireplace, and a cozy breakfast nook. A grand master suite was located on the first floor past the library, complete with a sunken tub in the modern bathroom and a walk-in closet that rivaled the one she had in New York. A private dining room, an office, a laundry room, and a powder room completed the first floor. Upstairs were three more bedrooms, two bathrooms, and a loft overlooking the living room.

"I left a lot of open space in the master bedroom so you can comfortably hold a crib, changing table, and one of those glider chairs when you're ready for babies," she said, matter-of-fact, as if she were in on plans that included more than the construction of the house.

Camellia eyed Henry, who appeared incredibly focused on the blueprints. "Uh, thanks," she muttered.

"If you're happy, I'll just need you to fill out some paperwork," she said, pulling a file folder from a worn briefcase. "I'll file the plans with the city, and once we have the permits, we can break ground."

"When do you expect the house to be completed?" Henry asked.

"As long as we stay on schedule, I would think you should be in by the end of September."

Camellia made a mental note to check the schedule for New York Fashion Week, which also took place in September. If things went as planned, she would need to be there to triumphantly watch Shelby walk in her first major shows.

When the comp cards arrived at her door via FedEx, Camellia was astounded to realize two weeks had passed so quickly. She had spent the time sifting through samples: siding and brick, shingles and windows, doors and wood floors, carpeting and lighting. She had already made many decisions for the house – Henry wisely leaving the complex design project in her capable hands – but there were still dozens to go, from the oversized stone tiles for the master bathroom to the white marble for the island in the kitchen. It was all consuming.

So when the strapping FedEx driver interrupted her wavering over the powder room sink to hand over her parcel, she welcomed the distraction. She sliced open the box, peeled back the flaps, and whooped joyously. Pulling on her boots and grabbing her fur, she grabbed a stack of cards out of the box, tucked them into a large envelope, and dashed to town, fervent to share with Shelby.

By the time she got within sight of the diner, Camellia was winded, but it was colliding with Shelby's mom outside the diner that took her breath away.

"Sharene!" Camellia exclaimed, steadying her footing. "Fantastic timing. I have Shelby's comp cards and she looks amaz–"

"Leave," Sharene hissed, causing Camellia to reel back. "Take those ridiculous cards and your fancy lifestyle back to New York and stay away from my daughter."

With jaw dropped, Camellia searched Sharene's drawn face for an explanation but all she found was loathing. "Sharene, I don't understand. I thought you and Shelby were going to move to New York together. The timing of selling the diner is so perfect."

"Is it?" Sharene's lips curled into a snarl. "You are so consumed with what you want, you never stop to see the affect your actions are having on everyone else."

Camellia was horrified. "Excuse me? What are you talking about?"

"I keep close tabs on my daughter. I know where she goes on dates and I know what magazines she reads. You singlehandedly destroyed *Flair* with your tunnel vision. It was all about you – to hell with the employees counting on a paycheck. You were going to do what you wanted to do, no matter the consequences. But not with my daughter."

Camellia took a deep breath, steadying both her anger and the whirlwind of dialog playing out in her head. "You misunderstand me," she said, having regained her composure. "I sincerely value your daughter. I would never hurt her."

"You already have."

"How?"

"By making her believe she has a future outside Markleeville."

"She *does*. Why are you so eager to keep her here?"

Sharlene's distorted face softened, turning downward like a bloodhound. "Because I need her more than you do." She opened the diner door and motioned Camellia inside.

Half an hour later, Camellia emerged from the diner, her eyes rimmed red. The dim gray light of the evening sky filtered downtown Markleeville, making it look as lonely as it felt. She stumbled along the sidewalk, not concerned with direction or the cold wind biting at her hands and face.

"Camellia?" The sound of her name pulled Camellia from her daze. She glanced around and saw Lisa standing in the doorway of her shop, waving her over, her expression one of concern. Camellia met her eyes and started to cry. "Hold on honey, I'm coming for you," Lisa called out, scurrying across the street. Upon reaching Camellia, Lisa put an arm around her shoulder and led her back to the store. "It's far too cold for man or beast out here today," she said. "A perfect occasion to dip into my brandy stash."

The store was empty, save for Deb, the owner of Do or Dye. Camellia recalled how she had practically run for her life from Deb's salon, making her cry harder.

"Sweetie, what is it?" Lisa asked, sitting Camellia in a chair next to the dressing room and disappearing into the back, reemerging in seconds with a brandy bottle and paper cups.

"I'm an awful person," Camellia sobbed into her hands. "An awful person with no life."

Lisa and Deb exchanged looks. "I think we're going to need more than a half-full bottle of brandy," Deb declared.

"We need Doc's," Lisa affirmed.

"And how."

The women grabbed Camellia's hands and pulled her to her feet. "I don't need a doctor," she insisted, as the tears continued to run down her face, cutting paths through her foundation.

"This one you do," Lisa assured, pulling Camellia out the back door and loading her into a red pickup truck. She climbed into the driver's seat, Deb jumped in on the other side, and Lisa took off, her tires spitting gravel in their wake. One stop down the interstate, they landed at Doc's Roadhouse.

Once the ladies had vodka in their glasses, and Deb convinced the bartender to leave the rest of the bottle on their table, Camellia started talking.

"I thought I had it all figured out," she said, frowning at her glass. "Shelby was my way back in. My redemption. She was going to take the modeling world by storm, and as the one who discovered her and molded her, I would be welcomed back into the society that had once shunned me."

"Why would you want to go back to them?" Lisa questioned, dipping into the bowl of salted peanuts. "They sound like a bunch of rat bastards."

Camellia cracked a smile. "They really are. Most of them, anyway."

"So why do you care?" Deb asked gruffly.

"I don't know," Camellia admitted, sipping her drink. "It doesn't matter now. Shelby won't be going to New York anytime soon. Sharene has breast cancer."

Lisa and Deb gasped. "Oh that poor woman," Deb said, shaking her head. "She's had it so tough, losing her husband so young, and having to raise a daughter by herself while running that diner day in and day out. How's Shelby taking the news?"

"To be honest, I'm not sure she knows. Sharene confronted me outside the diner, telling me I was taking her daughter from her. I don't think she was planning on announcing it." Camellia wiped at her nose with the bar napkin. "I didn't know," she whispered. "I really didn't know."

Lisa patted Camellia's hand. "Of course you didn't. How could you have? Fear makes us do crazy things, honey. From yelling at a perfectly nice stranger to putting all our hopes and dreams into one girl's modeling career."

Camellia stared at her drink. It was true. She had put her entire career in the hands of an eighteen-year-old girl. "I don't know what to do now," she admitted.

"You can be a friend to Shelby," Deb suggested in a kind manner. "She doesn't have many friends."

Camellia looked up at the women, stunned by this news. "Really? She's so friendly."

Lisa spit a piece of ice back into her glass. "You know how girls can be: gorgeous child, standing taller than everyone in her class, not a mean bone in her perfectly proportioned body."

"They shut her out."

Deb grabbed the bottle and refilled their glasses. "Like a stray cat."

"Which explains why she's so tight with her mom," Lisa continued. "Sharene was her only companion for years."

"And now?" Camellia asked.

"She's been dating Justin for a couple of years," Lisa said. "He's a good kid. Runs the family farm."

"And then she met you," Deb said, waving her glass at Camellia. "Never seen her happier."

Camellia's heart lightened at that. Until now, she hadn't considered that Shelby had become more to her than a client. But she had. She felt at ease around the girl, even able to let her guard down, to some extent, anyway. Shelby Jenkins may have been an unlikely friend – a young, small-town girl with no life experience – but she had become a friend just the same. And that friendship had been key in helping her adjust to Markleeville.

A thought stirred in Camellia and she glanced up at the two women, who were starting to look a little fuzzy through her buzz. "I've been kind of a shithead to you both. Why are you being so nice to me?"

Deb let out a whoop and slapped the table. "Sweetie, you were kind of a shithead, but Lisa and I don't operate by holding grudges. This is a small town. We have to stick together."

"Besides," Lisa added, throwing back the rest of her drink. "We know what you've been through. That would turn any of us into shitheads; at least temporarily."

Camellia cocked her head, her eyebrows furrowed. "You do?"

"Like I said, it's a small town," Deb said, signaling the bartender. "Who's up for another bottle?"

TWENTY-ONE

Camellia didn't remember much about getting home that night, but when she woke up the next morning, she was fully clothed on the couch, nestled under a faux-fur throw. She tried sitting up, but the sensation of being punched repeatedly in the head put her back down again. Her mouth tasted stale with a tinge of old vomit. She needed water, but there was no way she was going to try sitting up again. Her stomach felt like it had twisted around itself.

She tried closing her eyes to shut out the brightness, but lying there with her eyes closed made her nauseated, so she opened them again, covering part of her face with the blanket instead. *What time is it?* she wondered. *Where's Henry?*

There were footsteps on the stairs. Henry's footsteps, solid and rhythmic. "Henry," she murmured, placing a shaky hand on her pounding head.

"There's my party girl," he said brightly. "How's the head?"

She moaned. "Hurts."

"I'll bet. When the ladies carted you in here last night, you barely knew your own name."

"Deb and Lisa?" Camellia searched for the memory but came up empty. "They had to help me into the house?"

Henry retrieved a washcloth from a pile of laundry on the kitchen table. He wet it then placed it on Camellia forehead. "More like carried you." He sat on the edge of the couch and stroked Camellia's cheek.

"Stop it, that hurts," she whined.

He grinned. "I didn't know you made some friends. They seemed pretty nice."

"I hadn't. Not until last night anyway."

"So are they nice?"

"They're so nice." Camellia unfolded the washcloth and placed it over her entire face. "Henry, a lot has happened since yesterday."

"I can only imagine."

Camellia detected a hint of mockery and gave Henry a weak pinch on the arm. "I'm serious. I think life in Markleeville is about to change."

"Isn't that what you wanted?"

"Not like this."

By evening, Camellia's hangover had mostly subsided, save for a dull headache. She had managed to shower and get dressed, tying up her air-dried hair with a silk scarf. Henry, having left late for the hospital in order to first tend to his wife's disastrous state, was working late to stay on top of his patient load. To show her appreciation, Camellia decided to attempt a home-cooked meal of penne pasta with marinara sauce and crusty Italian bread. Her apron was spattered with tomato paste she had forced loose from the can, making her look like the loser of a bloody battle. With the sauce finally simmering on the stove, she filled a large pot with water, generously salted it, and set it on the back burner to boil, placing the lid firmly. She wiped her hands on one of the apron's few clean spots and sighed.

She had been in a state of melancholy all day. How much was due to the hangover, she couldn't say. But she guessed come tomorrow, when her body was once again clear of any residual alcohol, she would be feeling the exact same way. Sharene had breast cancer. Shelby would be devastated by the news. And she had nothing to look forward to except for a big, fancy house that suddenly seemed so garish and pointless.

She had known women who had nothing in their lives but their homes, from spacious apartments in the city to stretching summer homes in the Hamptons, and they threw themselves into making their spaces magazine-worthy retreats. They invented reasons to showcase their surroundings, from half-hearted dinner parties to hosting fundraisers, so other socialites would be forced into their homes to admire the splendor.

Camellia did not want that to be her future. But with her dreams of bringing Shelby to New York quashed, at least until Sharene had recovered, which could easily take a year or longer, Camellia had no clue what her future held. And this state of limbo felt like a vacuum, sucking her into nothingness.

The doorbell rang. Camellia put her hands to her head to check her scarf, forgetting about the signs of war on her apron, and opened the door. Shelby collapsed into her arms.

The sauce had burned and the pasta never made it into the water. Camellia sat on the sofa with the dirty apron still on, holding Shelby's head as the girl sobbed into her lap. Henry, who had arrived only moments after Shelby, added logs to the fire before driving two towns over to fetch Shelby's favorite Chinese food.

The three of them sat in a row on the sofa, working through their chicken fried rice in silence. The only sounds permeating the room were the clicking of chopsticks, the crackling fire, and Shelby's intermittent sniffles and quick catches of breath. And then, as if a switch had turned on, Shelby started talking.

"I should have known something was wrong," she whimpered, staring down at the take-out box. "She hasn't been herself for weeks. I let her convince me that some new diet was responsible for her weight loss."

"Is losing weight a symptom of breast cancer?" Camellia asked, trying to remember an article *Flair* had run on the topic a couple of years back.

"It is when it's spread to other parts of the body." Shelby began to cry again.

Camellia put an arm around the girl and pulled her close. "Oh Shelby, I didn't realize it was that advanced."

"Stage four. She never got it checked out. 'Too busy at the diner' was how she justified neglecting her health. And I just found out her aunt died of it. So it's in the family. It's in the family and she didn't get it checked out." Her swollen eyes managed to produce more tears, which Camellia wiped away with a tissue pulled from a full box wedged between them.

"I imagine her oncologist has recommended an aggressive treatment plan," Henry said.

Shelby blew her nose and dropped the wadded tissue into her lap. "Yes, but she's not doing it." She grabbed another tissue and held it against her eyelids, her body convulsing.

Camellia and Henry exchanged worried looks. "Why not?" Camellia questioned.

"She doesn't want it," Shelby stammered, as her body continued to shake. "She doesn't think it will make enough of a difference to go through it." She peered at Camellia through a red eye. "The cancer is in her bones now."

"Oh baby," Camellia cooed, rocking Shelby back and forth. She pushed away a strand of hair that was covering Shelby's face. "Would you like to stay here tonight?"

Shelby shook her head. "No, she needs me with her. I just don't want her to see me like this."

"Of course not," Camellia agreed. She looked up at Henry, who was clearing away their half-eaten dinner. "Would you get her some Ibuprofen and a glass of water? I'm going to get a few supplies and freshen her up a bit."

After Shelby had left, cleaned up but still looking physically worn, Camellia and Henry sat up in bed in the darkness, neither able to sleep.

"I keep wondering about the diner," Camellia mused. "Sharene's real reason for selling it. Was it to pay medical bills? Or to ensure Shelby had a nest egg to live off of after she's gone?"

"The only person who can answer that is Sharene," Henry said, adjusting his pillow and turning to face Camellia. "It's a sad situation."

"It's beyond sad. It's tragic. We have to do something, Henry. We have to help them."

"Agreed," he said, reaching for her hand. "What would you like to do?"

"If she doesn't get treatment, she's going to die, right?"

"Yes. Sooner rather than later. I don't blame her. When the cancer is that advanced, the only thing treatment is going to do is prolong her life, and there's no saying for how long. It can be a very painful and time-consuming way to spend your final months."

"Months? Is that all she has left?"

"I'm not an oncologist, but based on what Shelby said, that's my best guess."

She exhaled, staring up at the dim ceiling. "I think I know what to do." She smirked as the idea that came out of nowhere took hold of her. Just when she thought her future held no promise, she was proven wrong again.

TWENTY-TWO

Monday morning, just as Deb was flipping the closed sign to open, Camellia burst into Do or Dye. "I need a haircut," she pleaded.

"'Bout damn time, girlie." She led Camellia to the first chair next to the front window and tied a black cape around her neck. "You here for my Markleeville Mullet Special?"

"Oh yes," Camellia said, enjoying the sarcastic banter that Deb did so well. "A girl can't be all business all the time."

"So true. However, before I start chopping, what do you *really* want?"

"I want a pixie."

Deb gulped. "Really? You don't want me to shorten it in stages so it's not such a big change?"

"I want the change," Camellia said, studying her face in the mirror. "I need low maintenance."

"That's about as low maintenance as you can get." Deb shrugged her broad shoulders. "Okay, brave one, let's head over to the shampoo bowl, shall we?"

A half hour later, after cutting and gelling and blow-drying, Deb removed the cape and turned Camellia back to the mirror for the moment of truth.

"It's stunning," Deb said.

It was true. The super short haircut flattered Camellia's elegant bone structure. Camellia smiled widely into the mirror at Deb. "I love it," she said.

"Of course you do," Deb said, smugly. "This isn't that two-bit, buzz-cut factory next door," she exclaimed, facing the wall that divided the businesses and flipping off the barbershop with both hands. "This is Do or Dye!"

Camellia threw her head back and laughed at Deb's dramatic gesture. "Deb, honestly," she said, pretending to be stern with her.

Deb grabbed a broom and pushed Camellia's cut hair out of the way. "Is there anything else I can do for you today?" she asked.

Camellia set two twenties on the counter to pay for the fourteen-dollar haircut. "Actually, there is."

That evening, after Deb and Lisa had closed their businesses for the day, they met Camellia in the lot behind Lisa's Designs where Lisa's pickup was parked.

"Great hair!" Lisa exclaimed, promenading around Camellia to get a better look.

"I owe it all to Deb," she said sincerely, nodding in Deb's

direction.

Deb rolled her eyes. "Yeah, yeah, yeah, I can't take all this hero worship." She snatched the truck keys out of Lisa's hand and dangled them in front of Camellia's face. "Now, are we going to do this, or what?"

Camellia took a deep breath and closed her hand around the keys. "It's like riding a bike, right?"

"Sure," Lisa said, patting Camellia's back. "You're just a lot more likely to run down someone's bike with this truck."

The women climbed into the truck, with Lisa wedged in the middle and Camellia behind the wheel. Deb made a big show of fastening her seatbelt and bracing herself against the door. Putting the key in the ignition, Camellia gave it a turn and the engine roared to life. She looked around the interior of the truck with eyebrows furrowed. "How do I shift out of park?"

Lisa slapped at the steering column. "It's up here. Put your foot on the brake first."

"I remember that." She successfully put the car in drive – secretly thankful Lisa had backed in to the parking spot – and slowly maneuvered the car onto Beech Street.

"That's good, but next time you should probably come to a full stop and then look to make sure no cars are coming," Lisa instructed.

Camellia grimaced. "Sorry!"

"Lucky for you it's not tourist season yet," Deb chided, putting her hand up for a high-five from Lisa, which Lisa swatted away.

"Trying to teach here," she said sternly to Deb.

Deb gulped dramatically. "By all means, do go on. I'll just continue to hold on for dear life."

"Deb, you are *not* helping my level of confidence," Camellia griped. She made it through town without incident, turning right onto the second dirt road.

"Nobody will be on this street, so you can get a little more aggressive," Lisa said.

"Can I punch it?" Camellia asked eagerly, her eyebrows high.

"Can she punch it?" Lisa reiterated, nudging Deb's side.

"Why not?" Deb said, grabbing at the handle over the door. "Only live once, right?"

Lisa nodded at Camellia. "Go for it."

Camellia didn't need to be told twice. She pushed the gas pedal to the floor, making the old truck fishtail on the loose gravel. She let out a high-pitched whoop, holding the steering wheel at ten and two, as she remembered from driving school, and only letting up the gas enough to stabilize the truck as it sped along the dim, lonely straightaway.

"Balls to the wall!" Deb shrieked, laughing wildly.

"Better put a little more light on your surroundings," Lisa yelled over the roaring engine, reaching across the steering wheel and pushing back the brights lever.

The dim road flooded with light, illuminating the low, bordering cornfields and something moving in the road ahead.

"Deer!" Lisa wailed.

Camellia slammed the breaks and held tight to the wheel, fighting with the heavy truck that was pulling them off the road. The gravel under the tires slid the truck sideways. Someone screamed. A cloud of dust choked the evening sky. And then it was silent.

"Hell yes!" Deb cried, eye to eye with one of four white-tailed deer standing motionless in the road. She unbuckled her seatbelt and opened the passenger door, sending the animals prancing into the cornfield. "Oh sure, *that* makes you run, eh?"

"You can let go now," Lisa said, still in her seat, nodding at Camellia's white-knuckled grip on the steering wheel. "You did good. You did really good."

Camellia relaxed her hands. Her shoulders ached and her heart raced. "Wow, New York's got nothing on the treacherous driving in northern Michigan."

By the end of the week, Camellia was the proud owner of a used Escalade, purchased at Don Deacon's Cadillac located in Big Rapids. With all the wild beasts roaming freely around Markleeville, Camellia figured bigger was definitely better.

TWENTY-THREE

That Saturday, Camellia pulled up in front of the diner, emerging from her new SUV in black leggings, flat boots, and a black turtleneck. Spring had finally found its way to Markleeville, melting away the residuals of snow and dotting the trees along Beech Street with hopeful buds. Town was a little busier. Camellia learned from Deb that the seasonal business owners were arriving to prepare for the summer season, which included an influx of subcontractors already getting started on new construction projects.

Her own house was almost framed. While it was exciting, and required what felt like non-stop decision-making, it was now far from her focus, Camellia deferring to her husband to handle many of the remaining choices.

Once in the diner, Camellia sped past her usual seat at the counter, walking around to the other side and stowing her trenchcoat and handbag in a cupboard under the counter, as she had seen Shelby do dozens of times. Irene eyed her, started to open her mouth to say something and then closed it, turning instead to retrieve a side of mashed potatoes from the line. With potatoes in hand, she regarded Camellia again for a split second before disappearing into the back of the restaurant, presumably to devour the buttery dish.

Camellia yanked an apron off a hook behind her and put it over her head, wrapping the strings around her body and tying them in front. Shelby came out from the back and stopped in her tracks at the site of Camellia.

"What are you doing?" she asked, her face looking tired and strained.

"Working," Camellia responded, taking Shelby's pad and pen from her hands.

"Wait, did my mama hire you or something?"

Shelby's confused expression made Camellia smile. "No, I hired myself. And I'm firing you. At least temporarily."

"Did you buy the diner?"

Camellia laughed. "No, I didn't buy the diner. I'm just going to work here for a while. So you don't have to." She pulled at Shelby's apron strings, whisking the material over her head. "It's a non-paying position, of course. However, if anyone should take pity on me and leave a tip, it will rightfully belong to you."

"Camellia," Shelby whimpered.

"Hush now." Camellia picked up a full pot of coffee from the burner. "Your mama needs you now. The diner can wait." She moved along the counter, pouring from the pot and cleaning up discarded food.

"But Camellia," Shelby said, hurrying over to her, "what do you know about running a diner?"

Camellia set the pot down and crossed her arms. "I've been watching you do it since January. And don't worry," she said, twirling to grab the dishes the cook set on the line. "I won't run this place into the ground. I've learned a thing or two about making a business successful." She looked down at the dishes and then at the faces lining the counter that were looking curiously back at her. "Now, who had the Meatloaf Special and Turkey Feast?" she called out brazenly.

Camellia spent the better part of the summer going between the diner and the construction site, along with one long trip to the storage facility to trade out her winter clothing and boots for lighter, summery options.

She had gotten the hang of waitressing, even going so far as to proclaim to Henry that she had "missed her calling in the food services industry," inciting a laughing fit that rolled him off the bed. The small staff seemed to like her, too, and invited her to their regular Thirsty Thursday bar nights, which she attended when she wasn't too tired.

The diner was always packed now that summer was in full swing. The tourists changed over so frequently, just as Camellia had put to memory an entire family's names, they were gone, replaced with another excitable group ready for some downtime. There were many who came and stayed for large chunks of the summer, but they had their own kitchens and only ventured out to the diner for a night off from cooking.

Lisa and Deb had taken to having lunch there five days a week, as a show of support for Camellia. Lisa was an accomplished cook, and Camellia knew her friend's reheated leftovers were far superior to anything on the diner's menu. To show her appreciation for both their patronage and the lively talks they provided her each day, Camellia always slipped them a fresh piece of apple or blueberry pie – the one thing the cooks did very well – using her own money to cover the desserts once the ladies had finished their lunches and left.

The house was mostly complete on the outside, the gray shingled siding and steep dormered roof giving the home that charming Cape-Cod appeal. The screened-in sunroom at the back of the house on the first floor was turning into a peaceful space to enjoy a Sunday breakfast or read while watching the rain fall, while the open deck built over it, allowed for breathtaking views of the lake. Inside, the drywall was up, with the spackling and sanding stage in process. Now that the rooms were fully formed, Camellia and Henry could walk through the house and make their plans for paint colors and furniture placement. Even though Camellia had come to terms with living in the little cottage, she couldn't wait to have her own furniture again. The only thing she could wait for was getting to know her neighbors at the lake.

The topic of the lake residents had come up one afternoon in late

July over heated blueberry pie a la mode at the diner with Lisa and Deb.

"The foreman says we are still on schedule for an end-of-September completion," Camellia informed the women.

"I'm expecting one hell of a blow-out party," Deb said, dabbing a piece of pie in the melted ice cream at the bottom of the bowl.

Lisa raised her fork. "I'll second that. I'm also hoping for lots of invitations to drink a beer on that deck and watch the leaves change colors."

Camellia wiped at a stain on the counter with a wet rag. "Believe me, you'll be getting lots of invitations from me. I'm not expecting to find any friendly neighbors."

"You've already encountered The Snobs?" Lisa asked between bites. "They don't come into town much, thank God."

"Hey!" Deb cried out, elbowing Lisa in the arm. "You watch who you're talking about."

Camellia's eyes grew wide. "*You* live on the lake?"

Deb eyed Camellia seriously. "You suggesting I'm not fancy enough?"

"No, no, of course not–"

Deb broke into a laugh. "I'm just messing with you, Cammie."

It was the first time anyone besides Tray Mathers had used that nickname for Camellia. But where with Tray the name had sounded demeaning and childlike, coming from Deb it was actually nice. Camellia smiled sheepishly at the women.

"What is that goofy look for?" Deb asked, her eyebrows high.

"I don't know," Camellia started, suddenly embarrassed. She twisted the rag that was still in her hands. "I never had an easy time making friends."

"I thought big-time editors just paid people to be their friends," Deb joked, earning her another elbow from Lisa. "I'm starting to bruise," she complained, leaning away from Lisa's reach.

"Let the girl finish," Lisa scolded. She nodded in Camellia's direction. "Go on honey."

"When I was in high school I was completely absorbed with fashion, while the other girls were either boy crazy, horse crazy, or busy playing sports. I didn't fit in with them," Camellia explained. "Once I landed in fashion, I knew I had found my home, but it was more of a dysfunctional home rather than The Waltons." She sighed, chucking the rag under the counter. "Fashion is so competitive, and the higher up you get the more you wonder what people want from you. I could have an invitation to a dinner party every night of the week, but that wasn't because these people genuinely wanted to spend time with me. It was so they could get something from me, whether that was editorial in the magazine or a photo with them for Page Six. Not exactly my definition of friendship."

"So why did you go to their parties?" Deb questioned.

"It was my job. I have to stay on top of designers and models and photographers and everyone else in the industry. Socializing with them is the way to do that. But never, for one minute, could I let my guard down and share my secrets with any of them. I couldn't question my job or my boss of anything. Because the minute I share,

I know there's a damn good chance the information is going to spread through the industry like a virus."

"People love juicy gossip," Lisa agreed.

"Exactly. So I kept a professional distance."

"Has that changed now that you're not working in fashion anymore?" Lisa asked.

"No." Camellia lowered her eyes. "It's changed because I met the two of you."

Lisa reached for her napkin and held it over her face as her shoulders started to quiver.

Deb looked at Lisa and rolled her eyes. "Good God, Cammie, that kind of talk will have Lisa blubbering for the rest of the day."

"I'm okay," Lisa bellowed, causing Camellia and Deb to roar with laughter.

The bells over the door jingled and Camellia looked up to see Shelby helping a frail Sharene into the diner. The place fell silent save for the twangy country music coming from the radio. Camellia glanced around to see all the wait staff frozen, staring obviously. Even the cooks had come out from the back to have a look. It would be up to her to break the spell and return the diner to normal.

She rushed around the counter, giving a hug to Camellia then taking Sharene's slight hand into her own. "It's so good to see you both," she said enthusiastically. "Are you here to visit, or are you planning to stay for lunch, too?"

"I think just a visit," Shelby said, keeping a steady hand on her mom's back. "Want to sit mom?"

"Yes," Sharene said, her voice weaker than Camellia remembered.

"Pick your table and I'll bring you over some waters," Camellia instructed, hurrying behind the counter while scowling at the staff along the way, sending them back into motion. Once Shelby got her mom comfortable, waitresses and long-time patrons trickled over in small groups, giving careful hugs and words of encouragement. Camellia snuck around an elderly couple slowly working their way over to Sharene and set the waters on the table, motioning to Shelby to join her in the back. Shelby pulled a bottle of prescription medication from her jacket pocket, poured out two pills, and set them on the table next to her mom's water glass before slipping away to join Camellia.

Moments later the two were huddled together at the lone table in the cramped break room located at the very back of the building just beyond the dishwashing station.

"It's been almost a month since you've brought Sharene in. What's going on?"

Shelby sighed heavily. "She doesn't want to go anywhere. And she doesn't want me to go anywhere, either. The only time I get out by myself is to grocery shop, because she doesn't have the energy to walk that far and she refuses to use one of those scooters." Shelby slapped the napkin holder on the table across the room like a child having a tantrum. It clanged against the wall then fell apart as it hit the floor, paper napkins scattering everywhere. "I'm so sick of being in that house, Camellia."

"Is she worse? Could that be why she's hunkering down at

home?"

"Who knows? I have to beg her to get a morsel of information, and then sometimes I wonder if she's just making something up to get me off her back."

Camellia dropped her chin to her hand and frowned. "What does her oncologist say?"

"Beats me. It's my job to drive her, not to go into her appointment with her. I'm relegated to the waiting room, and then it's nothing but silence all the way home."

"I'm sorry honey. What can I do to help?"

Shelby gave Camellia a crooked smile. "You're already running the diner." She paused and cocked her head. "Did I hear you say 'hunkering'?"

"Shut it," Camellia said, faking a stern expression. "I've been spending way too much time with Lisa and Deb. Irene, too."

Shelby giggled, stooping to gather the strewn napkins into a pile. "You're turning into a real northerner," Shelby said. Camellia couldn't see her face, but she guessed Shelby was smirking. "Before you know it, your iTunes library is going to be filled with Rascal Flats and George Strait."

"Never," Camellia declared. "You can take the woman out of the city, but you can't force her to listen to wussy crap."

Shelby chuckled, pushing herself to a standing position, and placing the intact napkin holder back on the table. "Thanks Camellia." Shelby said. "I needed a laugh. It's been so long since I've had any fun, I'm starting to forget what it feels like."

"Seriously, Shelby," Camellia frowned, shrugging her shoulders, "there has to be *something* we can do. Would Sharene spend some time at my house? You both could come for dinner or just a lazy Saturday afternoon. Or, I could stay with her at your house and you and Justin could have some time together."

"Justin and I broke up," Shelby announced with a quivering lower lip.

Camellia caught her breath. "Oh no."

Shelby nodded. "He got tired of a relationship that had become all phone calls and texting." She sniffed loudly. "I can't blame him. Who knows how long this will go on?" She looked horrified. "Oh God, that sounded terrible! I'm terrible!"

Irene's plump frame appeared in the doorway, quickly stifling their conversation. Irene sized up Shelby's red face and frowned. "Your mama is looking for you. You better fix yourself up before you go out there so you don't upset her."

Camellia pulled a napkin from the dispenser and handed it to Shelby. "You relax," she commanded. "I'll think of something. I promise."

TWENTY-FOUR

"I promised her I'd think of something, but I can't think of one damned thing," Camellia muttered, as Henry's top half disappeared into the closet to find a tie.

"Between overseeing the house construction and running the diner, I'd say you've got enough on your plate right now." Henry emerged victorious from the closet, a pale blue and gold striped tie in hand. "You can't solve all of Shelby's problems."

Camellia raked her hands through her short crop. "Don't you get it, Henry? I've always been able to solve problems. That's how I moved up in publishing so quickly. *Flair* folding was the first time I couldn't fix something. I have no intention of that becoming a regular feeling."

Henry chuckled, finishing off an expert Windsor knot. "I've always loved you best when you're feisty, so who am I to stand in the way of hard core problem-solving?" He kissed Camellia on the head then scooped his phone and wallet off the top of the dresser. "In all seriousness, just be mindful not to step on any toes. Shelby still has a mom and I can guess Sharene won't take kindly to you acting as the super parent who can. Make sure whatever you do has Sharene's blessing." He moved to the doorway then stopped and turned, pondering a thought. "In fact," he said, tapping at his head, "I think you'll have the most luck if Sharene thinks the idea is her own. I *know* you know how to do that."

After Henry left for work, and the cottage was quiet again, Camellia went downstairs and opened all the windows, aching for a breeze on what was to be a near record-setting day for the first week of August. The silk slip she had slept in was already damp from the humidity. She poured a half-cooled cup of coffee and sat in front of the empty wood stove, which looked even more hideous without a lively fire rollicking inside.

It was hard to believe that in less than two months this tiny cottage would be a memory. She and Henry would have their expansive Cape Cod home on the picturesque lake. With central air, thank God. Things certainly had changed since they first moved to Markleeville eight months ago. She no longer longed for her job. She had fulfilled her desire for some purpose by running the diner, knowing she was allowing Sharene and Shelby valuable time they wouldn't otherwise have. However, it had become too much time for Shelby. The poor girl had looked so sullen at the diner the week before. Camellia loved seeing Shelby happy. Even more, she loved being the one who made her happy, from gifting her with beautiful handbags to guiding her towards an exciting career.

"Shelby still has a mom."

Camellia frowned, remembering Henry's words. When she first set eyes on Shelby, she had seen the girl as a means to an end – her celebrated route back to Manhattan and the inner fashion circles. She had seen herself as a mentor, as an agent, really, molding a fledgling girl into the star Camellia knew was within her. Certainly she hadn't thought of herself as a parental figure. Funny though, for how close she had become with Shelby, when she thought of her Markleeville friends, it was always Lisa and Deb who came to mind. Shelby wasn't part of that mix. She was different. Shelby was more. But more what? What *was* her relationship with Shelby? Camellia shrugged off the thought and trudged upstairs to get dressed. She wasn't going to make any progress staring at an old stove and daydreaming.

An hour later, Camellia was knocking at Shelby's door. After all this time, she had never been here before, and had to get the address from a reluctant Irene, fibbing that she was coming here to talk about employee raises. Shelby's surprised expression at finding her on the porch was exactly the reaction Camellia needed to pull off her half-cooked plan.

"Thank God you're here!" Camellia cried loudly, thrusting herself into the house. "Is Sharene here, too, I pray?"

"Of course she is," Shelby responded, her confusion apparent. "She's sitting in the sunroom."

"We all need to talk. Now."

Shelby led Camellia through the dim house to an old but meticulous screened-in porch where Sharene was resting on a wicker couch, propped up on colorful pillows.

"Sharene, I'm so sorry to bother you," Camellia said, taking the low wicker chair tucked in the near corner of the room. "I wouldn't have come if I could handle this on my own."

"What's wrong?" Sharene asked, her voice weaker than her concern.

"It's the cooks."

"Bryan and Martin are at it again?" Shelby asked, perching on the edge of the sofa, careful not to disrupt Sharene.

Camellia nodded emphatically. "Worse than ever. Bryan's threatening to quit if Martin doesn't start respecting him, and Martin's threatening to quit if Bryan doesn't start listening to him. They're both so volatile, I don't know what to do to appease either of them." She crinkled her forehead and bit her lip, attempting to convey the right amount of worry.

Sharene adjusted a pillow but didn't say anything. Camellia and Shelby sat in silence, waiting. After an uncomfortably long pause, Sharene turned her head in Shelby's direction. "You need to go make this right. We can't afford to lose those boys, no matter how big a pain in the ass they are. It's the end of the busy season. You can worry about replacing them in September."

Nodding, Shelby stood and adjusted the pockets of her shorts. "I'd better go right now. Camellia, would you mind staying with Mama until I get back?"

Trying not to smile and blow her cover, Camellia nodded back with the most solemn expression she could muster. "Of course."

Camellia could hear Shelby grab her keys and then the screen door swinging open and shut. Within seconds the truck engine fired up and then grew quieter as Shelby made her way down the street. Turning back to Sharene, she was surprised to find a sly smile on the woman's face. Camellia tilted her head in question.

"You're good," Sharene said, flatly.

"What do you mean?"

Sharene wagged a finger at her. "Don't be coy with me. I've been around long enough to know a decoy when I hear one."

"But Bryan and Martin..."

"Bryan and Martin have been fighting like spoiled brats for at least five years. I know you've enjoyed the spectacle more than once with the amount of time you've spent sitting at the counter. They've never quit and they never will. Who else would have them?" She struggled to lean forward. "So what's your real agenda?"

Camellia was speechless. She tried to find words, to explain herself, but they wouldn't formulate. Instead, she just sat there, her mouth half-open.

"Whatever it is, I know you don't mean any harm." Sharene signaled for Camellia to help her up, and Camellia scrambled to oblige. "Whatever your reasons are, you've been nothing but good to Shelby, and I can't thank you enough for that." Sharene inched her way to the kitchen with Camellia on her heels, her hands outstretched to grab Sharene if she should lose her balance. Once in the kitchen, Sharene sat in the closest chair at the table. Her breathing was rapid.

"Can I get you anything?" Camellia asked, softly.

"If you wouldn't mind, I would love a cup of tea. And my pain pills"

"Just point me in the right direction."

Camellia fixed two cups of Earl Grey, added a healthy dose of milk, and carried the steaming mugs to the table. She found the pills in an upper cabinet and set the bottle on the table, opening the lid. She knew Sharene was waiting for a response, and for all the excuses she was inventing in her head, she came to the conclusion that the truth was what Sharene deserved most.

"I'm sorry for the lie," she began timidly. "I'm worried about Shelby."

Sharene carefully lifted the mug and breathed in the fragrant aroma. "So am I."

"What are your worries?" Camellia asked, really wanting to know.

"I worry about what her life will be like when I'm gone."

"Is that why you put the diner up for sale?"

Sharene nodded, sipping her tea. "I didn't want her to worry about money."

Camellia fidgeted with her spoon. "Does Shelby want you to sell the diner? She seems to love that place just as much as you do."

"I don't know," Sharene said, grimacing. "I can't say I ever asked her." She fixed her gaze on Camellia. "And you? What are your worries?"

"I worry about what her life is like now."

Sharene set down her mug and knitted her brows. "Now?"

"Justin broke off their relationship because they never see each other."

"And that's my fault?" Sharene couldn't hide the defensiveness in her voice.

"No, of course not." Camellia was reevaluating on the fly her decision for total honesty. Perhaps, in the case of a frightened dying woman, a little fib was kinder than blunt truth. "Shelby loves you more than anyone, or anything, in the world. She doesn't want to leave your side for one minute. From the looks of her, that plan is taking a toll on her."

Sharene sighed and sat back, rubbing her eyes. Camellia couldn't be sure if she was tired or trying to restrain tears. "So what do you suggest?"

Perspiring from the heat – or perhaps it was the conversation – Camellia pushed away her tea and leaned forward on her elbows. "I suggest that you and I become friends. We spend some time together, giving Shelby opportunities to get out of the house and clear her head a bit." She smiled shyly. "I'm pretty good company."

Sharene stared hard at Camellia, as if trying to read her thoughts. "Why?" she finally asked.

"Shelby would never leave you alone, so knowing I'm here will make it easier for her to agree. And you said you were worried about what Shelby's life will be like. Justin could very well be an important part of her future, and wouldn't it be comforting to know that she had him to count on? To love her? They need a little time to be together. Just a couple evenings a week would probably do the trick."

"No." Sharene folded her hands in her lap and looked away.

Camellia was shocked. "No? You don't want this for Shelby?"

Sharene held up a hand and shook her head. "If you want to spend time with me, you're going to have to learn that sometimes I need a moment to catch my breath." She inhaled deeply and refocused her attention on Camellia. "What I was trying to say was no, that wasn't what I meant. When I asked you why, I was asking why this is so important to you. With everything you're already doing at the diner — and Shelby tells me you haven't paid yourself a penny, either — why are you willing to give more of your time to us?"

"Oh." Camellia pushed back the chair and stood, too restless to sit still any longer. She carried her half-full mug over to the sink, spilling out its contents and washing it. "When I first met Shelby, I knew exactly what she represented to me: opportunity, redemption. It wasn't until that opportunity was lost that I realized how much more she had become. I care for her very much."

"I know you do."

Camellia turned and leaned against the sink. "Even though I know she can't have everything, I want her to have every bit she can possibly have. I want her to have time with you. I want her to have the boy she loves. I don't want her to worry about the diner." She stopped, shrugging her shoulders. "Does any of this make sense?"

Two tears ran the length of Sharene's face. She nodded. "Perfect sense."

Watching Sharene cry made Camellia tear up, too. "Ooh, that sure is contagious," she said, ripping a sheet of paper towel and dabbing at her eyes. She tore off another and handed it to Sharene.

"I was awfully cruel to you, the day we first met," Sharene

murmured.

"You were coming from a frightened place. That's totally understandable."

Sharene wiped her eyes and balled up the paper towel. "Maybe. But what I said was completely untrue. And I'm deeply sorry for that."

Camellia closed her eyes, remembering so much of her former life: purposely ruining designers' clothing to prove she could; directing fashion editorials that few wanted to see; losing advertisers and never once caring; losing the magazine and only caring how it affected her; ignoring her parents at Christmas because she couldn't face them; leaving her apartment and knowing Trey had won; initially writing off the residents of Markleeville because they didn't meet her standards; being written off by The Snobs for reasons she couldn't comprehend; using Shelby to further her own agenda; the despair she felt when her golden ticket was torn in two; and Sharene's words – those harsh but truthful words that opened her eyes to the self-centered woman she had been for so long.

And through all of it, all the horrid decisions she had made in the name of art or business or self-preservation, there had been Henry, the handsome rock who remained steadily by her side.

She pressed her face into her hands. Facing the truth was hard. But at least her truth wasn't Sharene's. She had a lifetime to better herself, and make lots and lots of amends.

"Actually, Sharene, you were right on the money. And really, I should be thanking you, because you gave me the kick in the pants I desperately needed."

Sharene pushed back from the table, taking her time to stand. "I'll make you a deal. I'll keep kicking you in the pants if you promise to do the same for me. I don't want to get so wrapped up in my illness to forget my daughter's needs."

Camellia held out her hand. "Deal."

The screen door swung open, pulling the women from their handshake. Shelby appeared in the doorway, her expression perplexed. "Those boys were acting just fine to me," she said, a bit breathless. "Still, I told them not to cause trouble for you. I also threatened to stay open on Christmas," she confessed, grinning mischievously. "That drained the color from their faces, let me tell you."

"Nice work," Camellia said, giving Shelby a playful hug. "Well, I'd best be going. Sharene, I'll see you on Friday for card night."

"Card night?" Shelby questioned.

"Oh, yeah, Shelby, Camellia and I are going to hang out Friday night, if you don't mind."

"Oh," Shelby said, looking between the two women. "Me too?"

Camellia put a hand on Shelby's back as if to console her. "Um, if it's okay, Sharene and I were thinking just us two. Do you think you could find someplace to go for the evening?"

Shelby's joy was so palpable, Camellia could feel it emanating from the girl into her own body. "Yes! Yes, I'm sure I can come up with something."

Camellia stepped out into the blazing sun, sliding her oversized sunglasses into place. It was good to see a plan turn out the way it was intended. And there was still one more plan needing to be set into motion.

She pulled her phone from her handbag and speed dialed Northern Medical Center. When the receptionist at the main desk answered, Camellia's heart was racing so fast she had to lean into her SUV to steady herself. "Yes, can you connect me with a gynecologist on staff?" she sputtered. "I need to see about having my IUD removed."

TWENTY-FIVE

The first Friday evening with Sharene had exceeded Camellia's expectations. Sharene had appeared genuinely happy to see her, and they easily passed the time playing gin rummy, drinking iced tea, and getting to know each other. But it was Shelby's jubilant demeanor after returning home from her date with Justin that truly made Camellia's heart swell.

Camellia's own demeanor soured once she arrived home, however, when Henry greeted her by announcing that their presence was requested at another Diagnostic Radiology Services function. This time an end-of-summer cookout, back at the Farling home at the lake. Henry found the invitation amusing. Camellia did not.

"Look at it this way, we'll be outside for this party, so it'll be easier to run."

Camellia glared at her husband on her way to the kitchen, and grabbed a bottle of chardonnay from the refrigerator. "You can't honestly expect me to go through this again," she muttered, pulling the cork from the bottle and pouring half a glass. She swiveled back in his direction. "Could you?"

Henry met her at the counter and shrugged his shoulders. "I feel obligated to attend. I feel obligated to bring my wife." He picked up her wine before she could react and took a drink.

"Hey!" Camellia slapped at Henry's hand, causing the wine to splash onto the counter. "First you set me up, then you steal my wine, and then you *spill* it. Henry Rhodes, you're not having your best night." She plucked the glass out of his hand and slipped out of his reach. "If I wanted this level of insult, I could go down to the hardware store and spend time with that boy who refuses to call me anything but ma'am."

He followed her into the living room and wrapped his arms around her, kissing her on the neck.

"Henry, it's far too hot for you to be covering that much of my skin. We'd be better off doing that in a cold shower."

"Deal," he said, taking the wine from her hand again, this time setting it on the coffee table. "Let's go upstairs."

"Oh," she said, smiling shyly. "I'm sort of out of commission."

Henry did a double take. "You are? That hasn't happened since right after you had the IUD placed. Is everything okay?"

"Yeah." She sat on the arm of the couch and looked up sheepishly at her husband. "It's just not in there anymore."

"It fell out?" he gasped.

Camellia laughed heartily. "No, silly. I-I had it taken out."

Henry's face softened. "How come?"

Her bottom lip quivered for just a moment. "Because you can't get pregnant with an IUD."

He dropped to his knees and wrapped his arms around her legs. Camellia knew he wouldn't look at her because he was crying. She could feel it in the rapid motion of his back as it rose and fell.

Two weeks later, the last Saturday in August, Camellia and Henry returned to the lake, as ready as they were going to be for the cookout.

They passed their own house along the way, some of the construction crew working through the weekend to get the kitchen cabinetry installed. They would be living there in a month, and even though Camellia wasn't crazy about living amongst The Snobs, it was comforting to know that Deb would be only a quarter of a mile around the lake, an easy walk – or run – if necessary. And even though Markleeville had grown on her, and she liked having the downtown so close, she was ready to leave the cottage and its ugly wood stove, dreadful furniture, and microscopic closets.

They arrived at the party fifteen minutes early, with a grand plan to have some alone time with the host and hostess, David and Geri Farling. Camellia hoped a little friendly chatter before the other women arrived might break the ice and encourage Geri to show her a little warmth in the company of the other guests. A gesture that surely would be imitated if first done by the director's wife. Camellia hated the pretense but understood how cliques worked. And while she didn't have the slightest desire to befriend any of these women, they were tied to Henry's workplace, and the least she could do was try.

The party started much like the last one, except this time they met up with their hosts on the covered patio at the back of the house, which was set up with multiple tables that spilled onto the grass, signaling a sizable party. David was still unable to come up with Camellia's proper name, this time calling her Karina, and Geri once again managed thirty seconds worth of small talk before excusing herself to attend to a "situation." But this time, as the woman's slight figure disappeared into the house, Camellia followed.

"So Geri." Her voice was shaky; even more so when Geri came to a halt in the hallway, clearly surprised to find Camellia on her tail. "Um, how long have you and David lived here?"

Geri turned and looked down her nose at Camellia, scowling. "Three long years." Without waiting for a response, she swiveled and headed for the kitchen, Camellia continuing to follow.

"Where did you move from?"

Geri inspected a selection of cheeses on a sterling silver tray polished to perfection and shook her head. She placed her hands on the counter, leaning her weight into them, as if the condition of the cheese tray was more than her fragile disposition could handle.

"Thomas? Where's Thomas?" she demanded. The catering staff scattered out of the way as a short, stocky man with a pencil mustache stepped cautiously forward.

"Yes ma'am."

Geri bowed her head, Camellia assumed for maximum dramatic effect. "Thomas, didn't I say no Camembert? I seem to clearly remember specifying no Camembert, didn't I?"

Thomas looked at Camellia as if she might intervene at any moment. She gave a slight shrug of her shoulders in reply.

"Yes ma'am," he finally replied, shuffling his feet, "I believe you did say no Camembert."

"Then *why* is there Camembert on this cheese tray? Why?"

Camellia wondered if this was typical Geri or if her host was putting on a show for her. She was itching to intervene, to take the heat off of Thomas while making Geri look like the nutjob she was, but she was here to fall into favor with Geri, not humiliate the woman. So she remained silent and watched the performance that clearly wasn't over yet.

"Perhaps one of the catering staff confused it with the Brie, ma'am."

"Thomas, do I look stupid to you? Who confuses Camembert with Brie?"

Camellia felt the laughter rising from her chest into her cheeks, and she fought to suppress it, going so far as to fake a sneeze just to drop her head out of view for a second to hide her amused expression.

"I'll fix it myself, ma'am," Thomas assured, whisking the tray to the far end of the kitchen where he stood with his back turned. Camellia was sure it was so Geri wouldn't see him laughing, either.

Geri abruptly turned her attention back to Camellia. "Now, what did you want to know?" she asked sharply.

"Oh, um, I asked where you moved from."

"Chicago."

"A beautiful city," Camellia cooed. "I took many trips there when I was editing *Flair*."

"How nice for you," Geri replied coolly. "May I ask: have we begun a game of Twenty Questions? I have guests coming, you know."

Camellia's jaw dropped. She couldn't manage the forced pleasantries any longer. "I'm just trying to get to know you," she mumbled, humiliated.

Geri sighed. "This isn't the best time."

"Is there some reason that you don't want to know me?" Camellia questioned. Her fists clenched.

Geri checked her blue St. John sheath, which was perfect, and turned her head to the side, avoiding eye contact with Camellia. "I hear you're working at...a diner. Is that correct?"

"Yes, I am."

Turning back to look directly at Camellia, Geri clicked her tongue and shook her head slowly. "Apparently, David isn't paying your husband well enough. I'll be sure to have a chat with him about it. Now if you'll excuse me."

Geri stepped past Camellia, who had turned and raised a fist, trying to decide whether or not to strike. It was Thomas who made the decision for her, catching Camellia's hand and guiding it back down to her side.

"Won't do any good; she's icy to the core," he said in a hushed tone. "You'll only hurt your hand."

Camellia grinned and patted his arm. "Be sure to give me your card. You're my caterer for life."

He reached into his back pocket and pulled out a stack of business cards. "Excellent, maybe you can hire me to throw you a Camembert party."

Camellia laughed so hard tears ran down both cheeks. "Speaking of parties, I think this one is over for me. Good luck to you!" She breezed along the hallway and out the back door, spotting Henry sitting at a nearby table, surrounded by colleagues. They appeared to be engrossed in serious conversation, which meant most likely they were discussing a case. Camellia didn't want to disrupt him so she kept walking, pulling her phone from her bag and typing him a brief text message:

Pick me up at Deb's when you're done. No rush. XO

The laid-back atmosphere at Deb's comfortable A-frame house with its cool blue color palette was exactly what Camellia needed to decompress, which she did by kicking off her shoes, plopping onto the crisp white sectional, and putting back a frozen margarita courtesy of Deb's new power blender. Deb explained over the second margarita her good intentions for buying the blender.

"My sweet Charlie passed in 2003, and Lisa tells me six years is too long to be alone, so I figure I better drop a few pounds and get back in the dating game."

Camellia glanced around the living room, noticing a menagerie of framed photos featuring the same burly man with full beard and friendly blue eyes. "I didn't know you were married," Camellia said. "How did he die?"

"Aneurism," Deb said, tapping her head to indicate the location. "Real sudden."

Camellia put a hand to her heart, reacting to the dull pain that had found its way to her chest. She couldn't imagine losing Henry, especially so young.

Deb must have picked up on Camellia's distress, because she elbowed her then and clinked her glass. "It was a long time ago. I'm fine. As a matter of fact, I'm not even sure why I'm considering dating. I haven't had a problem with my life. Lisa's the one who's forever worried about me living out here alone."

"Lisa wants everyone to be happy," Camellia acknowledged.

"I *am* happy," Deb insisted. "Or at least I was. Now that I've got dating on the brain, I'm turning stupid. For God's sake, I blew two-fifty on that stupid blender to make juices and smoothies so I could lose a couple of pounds."

"You're not that stupid," Camellia needled. "The thing makes incredible margaritas."

Henry rapped on the door as the third round of margaritas were getting polished off. On Deb's insistence, he joined the ladies at the kitchen table, where they had moved to be closer to the blender.

"Your house is charming, Deb," Henry said, looking around and nodding. "How long have you lived here?"

"Four years," she said, pushing her glass across the table, appearing to be done. "Before that, Charlie and I had a ranch in town." She peered at Henry, said "He passed," and fixed her eyes on Camellia, obviously not caring to go over the details again.

"What made you want to live out here by yourself?" Camellia asked, resting her cloudy head on Henry's shoulder.

"It was different. I needed something different. If it wasn't for The Snobs, this place would be perfection."

Camellia picked her head up and turned to Henry. "Speaking of The Snobs, how was the rest of the party?"

"Manageable," Henry said, rubbing his wife's back. "I take it from your text things didn't go so well with Geri."

She threw her head back and laughed. "That's an understatement. I don't think things will ever go well with Geri. Or any of those women, for that matter. I don't know what their problem is with me."

"I do," Deb said, getting up to root in the pantry for snacks.

Camellia and Henry exchanged a puzzled look. "You do?" Camellia asked.

Deb emerged from the pantry with a bag of Doritos. "Sure. You adapted."

"Adapted...you mean to Markleeville?" Henry asked, still looking bewildered.

"Exactly. They don't like that." She tore open the bag, spilled some of the chips onto the table, which was apparently filling in for a bowl, and took a handful, munching loudly. "See, none of them wanted to come here, just like you. But while they clung together, relishing in their misery, and hoping all the doom and gloom will be the catalyst to their spouses finding jobs elsewhere, you gave Markleeville a chance. That's like the kiss of death."

"Wow," Camellia said, giving in to the chips and snagging the few closest to her. "That makes a hell of a lot of sense."

"I have to admit, it really does," Henry conceded, shifting in his seat and crossing a leg. "But Deb, how do you know all this?"

"A group of them power walk past my house every evening in good weather," Deb explained, one hand filled with another round of chips. "And lord can they *talk*. It became sport to eavesdrop. You can't imagine how many times I weeded the same little plot of land in my front yard, just to listen to those baboons babble."

Henry had to hold Camellia upright as she shrieked with laughter.

TWENTY-SIX

Once Labor Day weekend had passed, the town of Markleeville wound down from a touristy roar to an early off-season hum, with some of the older part-time residents, who no longer had to rush down state to get their kids back to school, staying on a bit longer to relish the quieter side of summer.

Meanwhile the last of the detail work was in full swing at Camellia and Henry's lake house: carpeting was being laid, the remaining light fixtures were getting installed, a re-ordered marble countertop was being secured into place. With the patio finally in place, the landscapers were due out that week to install sprinklers, grass, and a lush grouping of shrubs and trees.

Now that the diner had finally slowed down, Camellia was able to take an extra day off during the week, which she used to give Shelby an additional afternoon out of the house. While there were a hundred other things she could have done with that time, especially packing their things at the cottage and measuring for window dressings at the new house, Camellia didn't mind. She knew Sharene was getting weaker, and she wanted to take advantage of the time she could spend with her newest friend.

However, Camellia was shocked to discover Sharene looking energetic and happy when she arrived for a Wednesday afternoon visit.

"Isn't it amazing?" Shelby remarked, grabbing her shoulder bag and keys from the chair nearest to the door. She hugged her mom and held Sharene's face in her hands. "She woke up like this, all sparkling and lively. Sure looks like remission to me!" She kissed her mom on the forehead and then grabbed Camellia, bestowing a bear hug. "Be back soon, have fun!"

Camellia and Sharene watched Shelby drive away, making sure she was out of sight before Camellia closed the front door and pulled Sharene onto the couch. "Do you think you're in remission?"

Sharene grinned sardonically. "No. But Shelby can think it all she likes. I can't remember the last time I saw her in such high spirits."

Camellia pressed her lips together and knit her brow. "So what do think it is?"

"I did a little research while Shelby was in the shower this morning. There's a lot of talk out there about one last burst of energy before dying."

Slack-jawed for a moment while digesting the information, Camellia shook it off and frowned at Sharene. "Well, if that's the case, shouldn't you be spending this time with Shelby?"

Sharene crinkled her nose. "I don't want her to know. Besides, I could be wrong, right?" She patted Camellia on the knee. "Come with me. I have something for you."

Following closely behind, Camellia climbed the stairway to the second floor and then ascended another narrower set of steps hidden behind a door. It led to a crowded attic that smelled of cedar and mothballs.

"Over here, by the window," Sharene called out, bending over a row of old packing boxes that had softened with age.

"What is it?" Camellia wondered aloud, expecting Sharene to bring out old family photos to show her.

Instead, Sharene held up a spectacular black trench coat with a detachable shawl cape. Camellia stood dazed, feeling pretty sure she knew exactly what she was looking at. "Is that...Yves Saint Laurent?"

Nodding, Sharene said, "From the '70s. It was my mother's."

"M-May I?" She could barely speak. Sharene placed the coat in her arms. Inspecting it carefully, Camellia's eyes continued to widen. "It's perfect. No wear."

"She was quite the collector in her day," Sharene explained, opening each of the boxes in front of her and pulling out armfuls of vintage clothing; the sight of them making Camellia gasp. "My father was a defense attorney in Chicago," she went on. "Had a lot of high profile cases, which made him a lot of money. My mom always knew how to spend it."

"Does Shelby know?" Camellia couldn't believe such a treasure had been sitting untouched in this attic for years, possibly decades.

"Sure," Sharene said, unfolding a Chanel pantsuit with wide, cropped legs. "Unfortunately, she's way too tall. My mom was only about five-foot-four." Camellia gasped again as she took the fitted Chanel jacket from Sharene's hands, running a hand across the gold-button detailing. "I thought you could find some use for them."

Camellia whipped her head up to look at Sharene. "You're...giving them to me? But they're so valuable."

"You're valuable." With only minor trouble, Sharene lowered herself to the dusty floor and sat cross-legged. "You've done so much for Shelby and me. So much. This is the least I can do."

Peering through the contents still in the boxes, Camellia exhaled heavily, taking it all in. "I'm not sure how much of it will fit me, either. I'm on the taller side, too."

"Actually, I thought it would be a nice start for your own vintage boutique."

"A vintage boutique?"

"I don't know how much of it would sell in Markleeville, but I'll bet you could have some success online."

Camellia leaned against the windowsill and gazed down the quiet, tree-line street, pondering the thought. She adored vintage clothes. And she certainly knew her designers. There would be a bit of a learning curve, figuring out how to price the items, but that could quickly be remedied with enough research, which she was willing to do. She fingered the hem of the Chanel jacket she was still holding. She did have a website she wasn't using for anything now that the modeling agency idea was kaput. With a few instructions, her web guy could turn it into a shopping site. Maybe she could write a weekly column for it, too, educating shoppers on the eras and the designers and what to watch out for when shopping vintage. Henry could photograph the clothing. And she could run the business from home, which would be convenient if there was a baby.

She turned back to Sharene, who was staring at her intensely as if willing Camellia to say yes. "I can't thank you enough," Camellia gushed. "I want to do it. I want to have my own online boutique."

"Thatta girl." Sharene smiled brightly, and held up a hand. "Now help me up, would you? I want to save some energy for Shelby."

TWENTY-SEVEN

On Monday, Camellia and Henry met with the builder and his sales rep for the official walk-through. Room-by-room they turned on lights, flushed toilets, opened and closed windows, and checked faucets and drains. Henry kept a keen eye on paint finish and nail holes, while Camellia made sure all their choices were accounted for. The house felt vast at this stage, with the rooms finished but not yet furnished. With the exception of a few minor fixes, including one set of lights wired to the switches in the wrong order, the home was perfect. The sales rep marked up the paperwork, indicating the changes needed, and Camellia and Henry signed off.

They were scheduled to close on the house on Thursday, giving the builder plenty of time to make the repairs and clear out. Camellia booked the moving company for Friday morning, but she and Henry were planning to spend Thursday night there, with carryout and a makeshift bed on the floor. It had been Camellia's idea. She had waited a cycle after having her IUD removed to try to get pregnant, and she had a romantic notion of conceiving that first night on the floor with nothing else present but the two of them.

After the builder left, Camellia and Henry walked out to the back patio to watch a large flock of geese feeding on the vegetation by the water.

"They're getting ready for winter," Henry noted, as a smaller flock flew overhead.

"I feel like we are, too," Camellia said, sliding her arm around Henry's back. "No more ugly wood stove."

"No more country-blue, overstuffed furniture," he added.

"And I was worried you would attempt to take it with us," she teased, reaching up for a kiss. Her cell phone rang and she let go of Henry to dig for it in her oversized tote. "It's Shelby," she announced brightly.

Shelby's low wail eradicated Camellia's smile. Her pained expression revealed everything to Henry, and they bolted for the car with Henry behind the wheel and Camellia pressed against the passenger door, ready to run to Shelby. Her foot tapped the floor wildly. Neither of them spoke.

The tires squealed as Henry took the turn onto Shelby's street. He pulled into the driveway, and Camellia leaped from the Escalade before Henry could come to a complete stop. She tore through the front door, following Shelby's cries upstairs.

She halted in the doorway of Sharene's bedroom. Sharene was laid out on the made bed, her arms at her sides, her face peaceful. Shelby sat on the floor at the foot of the bed, rocking from side to side, her shoulders heaving.

"I'm here," Camellia called out. Shelby jerked around and peered at Camellia with red, swollen eyes, and then scrambled into her arms. They stood in the doorway for what felt like hours, Camellia holding the girl tight as Shelby sobbed into her shoulder. Henry appeared quietly, surveyed the scene, and touched Camellia on the small of her back. "I'll call the funeral home," he whispered, and then disappeared downstairs.

When the funeral director arrived, Camellia and Shelby were seated in the living room, Camellia feeding a steady stream of tissues into Shelby's hands. Henry was waiting outside, and held the door open for two solemn-looking men, who expressed their condolences to Shelby in hushed tones before following Henry upstairs. Within minutes they were carefully making their way back down, reverently managing the weight of the body bag they carried between them.

At the sight of the body bag, Shelby hid her face in the crook of Camellia's neck, wailing uncontrollably. Tears slid down Camellia's cheeks, which she whisked away with the back of her free hand. She was more crushed by Sharene's death than she had expected, but this wasn't the time for her to break down. Her job was to be strong for Shelby.

While Henry sorted out details with the funeral director, Camellia took Shelby up to her room to help her pack a bag. She refused to let Shelby stay in the house alone that night.

"Tomorrow you can decide what you'd like to do, but for tonight, you're coming with us," Camellia instructed gently, pulling a couple of outfits from Shelby's closet and folding them into a pile on the bed.

Shelby nodded weakly. "I wish she had fought harder," she mumbled, the first words she had uttered since calling Camellia.

Camellia clicked her tongue, dropped the dress she was holding, and put her hands on her hips. "Don't ever let me hear you speak of your mother that way again. She fought her whole life. She raised you single-handedly and *ran* a successful diner to provide a good life for you. She even fought against severe treatment so she could enjoy every last minute with you. Your mother was a fighter, Shelby. And one day, you'll realize that you are, too."

A chilly northern wind greeted Camellia and Shelby as they stood in front of the diner early Thursday morning. Beech Street was as quiet as Camellia had ever seen it, with every business closed and the Escalade the only vehicle parked along the street. Camellia turned the lock and pushed open the diner's front door, the tinny bell ringing like a gong against the reticence town.

Hesitantly, Shelby followed her inside, gripping onto a small sign they had come to adhere to the front door, announcing the diner would be closed that day for a funeral and private luncheon. Camellia flicked on the lights, looked around, and gasped.

The perimeter of the diner was lined with photographs, three and four rows high. Camellia and Shelby looked at each other with wide eyes and pushed slowly forward, taking in the scene. While Camellia didn't recognize many of the people, she knew what she was looking at: it was the story of the Beech Street Diner, staring Sharene and Shelby.

Sliding into one of the booths, Shelby scanned a grouping of photos taped to the wall, giggling lightly.

"What is it?" Camellia asked, moving closer for a better look.

She pointed to a photo in the bottom row. "I remember this day," she murmured.

The picture was of a young girl, about five, standing on the diner counter wearing an apron that stopped below her feet. She was holding two ladles high over her head, her expression fierce.

Camellia grinned. "I take it that's you."

"I told my mama I was quitting kindergarten and working at the diner instead." Shelby threw her head back and laughed. "I thought the diner was way more fun than sitting in a circle reciting the alphabet."

Camellia's eyes locked on a faded photo of a beautiful young couple locked in an embrace, smiling widely for the camera. "That must be Sharene. She looks just like you."

"And my dad," Shelby added, lightly running a finger across their faces.

"You had no choice but to be gorgeous with such stunning parents," Camellia noted, which Shelby didn't seem to hear. She looked lost in thought as her eyes moved from one old photo to the next. "I'm going to put on some coffee," Camellia murmured mostly to herself. As she reached the counter, she noticed an envelope lying there with Shelby's name on it.

"I wonder who did all this?" Shelby's wistful voice floated across the diner.

Camellia waved the envelope in the air. "Perhaps this will shed some light on it."

Shelby cocked her head and padded across the checkerboard floor, gingerly taking the envelope from Camellia. She tore it open and removed a sympathy card that had been signed by all the employees. She read aloud, slowly and deliberately.

"Shelby, it's been an honor working for Sharene for the last twenty years and it would be an honor to work for you twenty more. We love you and stand beside you: the Beech Street Diner staff."

Shelby hugged the card, her expression an unmistakable look of pride.

The tinny bell announced Henry, Lisa, Deb, and Justin, all of them crammed in the doorway. "It's time," Henry said.

Shelby's doleful sigh reset the somber mood. With downcast eyes, she shuffled to the door where Justin put an arm around her and escorted her to the car.

"Where you able to get the closing moved?" Camellia asked Henry quietly, locking the diner behind them.

"Rescheduled to three o'clock. The luncheon will be over by then, and Lisa and Deb said they'll stay with Shelby until we're done."

As Henry pulled out into Beech Street, following behind Lisa's truck en route to the chapel at the cemetery a mile and a half north of town, Camellia looked back at the diner. So many good memories were wrapped up in one little space. Some started years before Camellia had ever heard of a sleepy little town called Markleeville, back when she was still fighting to flee small-town life for something bigger. And some happened just this year, like the day she set eyes on a fresh-faced Shelby Jenkins.

And it was meeting Shelby and realizing that a trusting young girl filled with potential could become so much more than a power play – could, in fact, fill a childless void Camellia hadn't even know existed – that she had found something bigger than all of New York City. And when she added Henry and Lisa and Deb and Sharene and all the characters, both good and bad, who made up Markleeville, what Camellia had found was a home.

EPILOGUE

"Shelby, look at this!"

Camellia held out an arm, adorned with green and yellow bangles.

Shelby cut through the thick crowd of shoppers to inspect the find. "Pretty," she said, brightly, examining the smooth, colorful resin. "Are they good pieces?"

Looking around them first to ensure no one was listening in, Camellia nodded, keeping her voice low. "They're Bakelite. Very collectable."

Noticing a similar bangle in red mixed in with a pile of beaded necklaces, Shelby plucked it up and slid it onto her arm. "This one, too?"

Camellia ran her fingers repeatedly over the bangle Shelby was wearing and sniffed the scent. "Yes."

"You can tell by smelling it?" Shelby's look suggested she was questioning Camellia's sanity.

"Yes, it's one of a few ways to tell. Come on, we're taking them all. Don't let on that we think they're anything more than cheap costume jewelry. Most vendors at flea markets have no idea what they're selling and we want the lowest possible price."

Bending down to gather the bags at her feet, Camellia felt a dull pain in her low back and groaned lightly.

"Are you crazy?" Shelby asked, clicking her tongue. "Get out of the way and let me get them." Her long hair whipped across her face as she scooped up the hodgepodge of accessories they had purchased from a handful of vendors at the other end of the mammoth tent.

"Please, I'm pregnant, not an invalid."

"Three months from now, you can lift your car, if you want. But until that baby comes out, consider me your personal bellhop."

As Shelby pulled a bag onto the crook of her arm, the tiny diamond on her left hand glistened in the light. Camellia was relieved when Shelby explained it was a promise ring and not an engagement ring. While Justin would surely make a fine husband one day, Camellia didn't want Shelby to rush into marriage. It was easy to understand wanting to hold tight to something good after experiencing a substantial loss. That's precisely why she and Henry insisted that Shelby come live with them at the lake. They didn't want her to endure the loneliness she was feeling in her childhood home, or have financial worries for both the diner and maintaining a house on her own. They were the types of emotional fragilities that could make a person do something she wasn't ready for or didn't fully want. Especially at Shelby's age.

Once Shelby had taken the time to grieve Sharene's death and determine what she truly wanted to do with her life, Camellia knew she would step back and let the young girl fly. But until then, she and Henry would be there to support and guide her.

Shelby's text alert beeped, and with her free hand, she maneuvered the phone from the front pocket of her jeans and scanned the message. "Good news," she said, turning sideways to escape a flock of teenage girls shrieking over a stack of one-dollar DVDs. "The realtor got me a renter for the summer. They'll be in the week after school lets out."

Camellia let out a whoop. "Shelby, that's fantastic! Now give me a moment to do my thing, and we can head home to celebrate."

After a fervent round of negotiating with the vendor, Camellia emerged from the stall victorious, waving her bag of bangles in the air.

"Let's get out of here," she said, shuffling toward the parking lot, which looked busier than Times Square. "I want to get all the new stuff priced, photographed, and uploaded to the website by the end of the week. It's supposed to be summer-like this weekend, and I want my parents' first trip to Markleeville to be primarily spent on the patio, with virgin piña coladas and juicy grilled steaks – my latest cravings."

Shelby huffed, loading the packages into the back of the Escalade. "Save some for me. I scheduled myself at the diner all day Saturday so Irene can go to her son's wedding in Detroit."

"You're a good boss," Camellia said, hiking her extra weight into the driver's seat. "I'm glad you decided to keep the diner. I can't imagine anyone else owning it."

"Neither could I." Shelby flipped open the visor mirror and checked her lip gloss. "When is your story due for *Vanity Fair*?"

"Not for another week. It's only three hundred words; I could write that in my sleep. Especially when the topic is vintage."

"It's a start." Shelby took over the radio, landing on a guitar-heavy anthem she immediately turned up, and Camellia swiftly turned back down. *God, I'm getting old*, Camellia thought, laughing to herself.

Camellia looked over at Shelby, who was singing along to the song, her head and long legs bouncing up and down to the driving beat. Feeling a kick of her own, her hand went instinctively to her swelling belly, her bracelet from Henry jingling with a new baby carriage charm.

Pressing her foot harder on the gas pedal, Camellia navigated her way along the winding road – brilliantly lined with the yellow-green hues of late spring – leading back to Markleeville. The next chapter of her life was waiting.

ABOUT THE AUTHOR

Karen Buscemi has been writing professionally for 16 years, with articles published in Women's Health, Self, The Huffington Post, Figure, Successful Living, The Detroit News, plus a number of metro Detroit magazines. She is the editor of StyleLine magazine, a style magazine based in Michigan.

Karen is also the author of *Split In Two: Keeping It Together When Your Parents Live Apart* (Orange Avenue Publishing/Zest Books, March 2009), a self-help book for teens shuffling between houses; and *I Do, Part 2: How to Survive Divorce, Co-Parent Your Kids, and Blend Your Families Without Losing Your Mind* (Norlights Press, February 2011).

ACKNOWLEDGMENTS

Gobs of gratitude to:
Jim Benton, Susan Shapiro, Nicole Bokat, Camille Noe Pagán,
Matt and Allison Malmstrom, Theresa and Mark French,
Kelly Johnson, Emilia Delena, and Raffaella Naurato.

And, of course, my crazy-amazing family:
Frank Buscemi, Noah Correll, Jesse Buscemi, and Margaret Shulzitski